MW00773645

# Broomstick Blend

A Paramour Bay Mystery
Book Eight

KENNEDY LAYNE

**BROOMSTICK BLEND**

# DEDICATION

Jeffrey—A home generator was the best idea…no power outages!

Cole—If you truly believe, it will come true!

*A baffling whodunit arises while comical antics abound as USA Today Bestselling Author Kennedy Layne continues her Paramour Bay Mysteries...*

Lady bugs, bumblebees, and butterflies are enjoying the humid summer days and nights in the quaint Connecticut coastal town of Paramour Bay. Completely exhausted, Raven Marigold is doing everything she can to keep her cool after the town mysteriously loses power. No electricity means no coffee...no coffee means that Raven's nerves are more than a bit frayed.

After a bit of investigating, Raven discovers evidence that witchcraft might have been involved in causing the power outage that has puzzled the residents and left them a little bit cranky. Well, their irritability turns into straight up panic when a possible murder victim is discovered smack dab in the middle of the town's cobblestone square.

Bring a flashlight if you want to help Raven and the rest of the gang solve this latest blackout mystery that will have you scrambling to turn the pages until the very last sentence!

# Chapter One

THE SMALL COASTAL town of Paramour Bay, Connecticut was quaint, unique…and currently, extremely hot. A heat wave of epic proportions had descended upon the area, sending the temperatures soaring into the high nineties with virtually no breeze off the bay. To make matters worse, a power surge had occurred in the main electrical grid that fed the Connecticut coastline last night, and the entire town had fallen prey to the blackout…that is, anyone without a generator and fuel.

Normally, events like this one weren't too much of a big deal and the power usually returned in a few minutes.

This time?

Not so much.

It was now going on two o'clock the following afternoon with no relief in sight. That's right…we were going on fourteen hours without the benefit of electricity. That didn't stop the owners of the mom and pop shops on the main thoroughfare of town from flipping their welcome signs and opening their front doors to whoever wanted a brief respite from the blazing hot sun.

Including me—Raven Lattice Marigold.

I was the owner and proprietor of a charming tea shop in Paramour Bay called *Tea, Leaves, & Eves*. The charming town sat comfortably on the southern coastline looking out over the Long Island Sound. We usually enjoyed a lovely breeze that came off the water in the later afternoon, but even the elusive southwestern onshore winds had deserted us.

I found myself counting my blessings, in that it was a good thing I had received a delivery of inventory yesterday to steep the perfect combination of tea leaves for a deliciously unique sweet tea blend. The oversized glass jars were currently sitting on high-top tables just inside the entranceway to lure the patrons in for a sample. What little ice I had left from a large five-pound bag I'd gotten from the gas station had melted hours ago.

*I'm dying.*

"You're not dying, Leo," I mumbled from my draped position at the counter, allowing the battery-operated fan in front of me to rotate a weak imitation of a breeze over my face as it panned to and fro. There was no keeping the drips of perspiration from rolling down my cheeks from underneath my hairline, but the slight movement of air was better than nothing. "You have your fresh bowl of water and my only other battery-operated fan. I heard that the power should be restored soon."

I'm not hearing voices, I swear.

*How do you know it's not the delirium from heatstroke?*

"Because you've been a thorn in my side for much longer than the power has been out," I countered irritably, wondering if there was any cold left that had been trapped inside the malt shop's deep freezer next door. There could be worse places to hide out until the power came back on. "Plus, I'm pretty sure that I wasn't the one who made all those online purchases of premium organic catnip on my credit card."

*Are you sure? I've seen you sleepwalk before, you know.*

I guess I should explain exactly who I was carrying on a conversation with these last few minutes. It wasn't because I had been deprived of my coffee today, either. You see, the voice only

I could hear inside of my head was actually my familiar.

Well, technically Leo had belonged to my grandmother. He'd been left behind to mentor me.

Nan had been adventurous enough—okay, maybe a bit careless, too—to use a necromancy spell to keep Leo from crossing over into the afterlife with her. She'd wanted him here to help me adjust to my new way of life as a practitioner of the mystic arts, but there were some pretty harsh consequences for dabbling in such dark magic.

With that said, I'm almost certain Leo's flair for the dramatic had already been ingrained in him from the start. He certainly hadn't acquired his snarky behavior by aging gracefully.

*The definition of dramatic was you telling me that we'd have our air conditioning working by this morning. You lied, and now I'm going to die from heatstroke. Don't invite Skippy and his band of ninja squirrels to my funeral. I don't want him to know I died in such a dishonorable death. Maybe you could circulate a story that I suffered from Post Traumatic Squirrel Disorder.*

Let me catch you up to speed—the Marigolds happen to be a family of witches.

I didn't find out until I'd moved here last October, so you can imagine my surprise to discover that I had the ability to cast magic spells. My mother, who is entirely another story for a later time, thought it best to keep me in the dark about the skeletons in our familiar closet—no pun intended. Thinking back, my thirtieth birthday was the day that my life had been turned upside down and I'd finally found a place to call home.

*Where? The deepest depths of Hades?*

"Beetle should be here soon," I reminded Leo, trying to get his mind off the fact that he had a very thick coat of tangled fur. I was so tempted to try another call to my part-time employee on his ancient cell phone. He'd been gone for hours, in search of more ice from a vendor who hadn't been cleaned out this morning. I'm pretty sure that the majority of the residents had already bought every bag of ice there was within a thirty-mile radius of Paramour Bay, but Beetle still shouldn't have been gone for this long. "I'll put some ice cubes in your water bowl the second Beetle walks through that door."

*I'll be dead by then. Do you have a notepad handy? I should probably pen my last will and testament.*

I didn't bother to reply to Leo this time, who was currently flopped on his back with his paws stretched out toward the ceiling in the middle of the tea shop. The small battery-operated fan barely moved his fur, and his tongue was peeking out the side of his mouth.

Oh, and that little necromancy spell I'd mentioned a bit ago?

It had done a number on his physical appearance. Seriously, his black fur now had splotches of an odd orange color. His whiskers were bent, his tail was crooked, and his left eye had a tendency to bulge out more than his right when he was stressed. On top of all that, his munchkin legs somehow managed to carry his somewhat oversized body, which was quite a few pounds heavier than it had been before going through such a dangerous life-altering spell.

*My weight is the least of my worries. I can no longer feel my tail, Raven. It's gone numb once again. There's not even the slightest tingle left in that poor wretched appendage. I thought that symptom only came with hypothermia or one of your more poorly worded spells. Clearly, I've been permanently transmogrified.*

"Leo, your tail is resting in your water bowl, and I'm not sure that is even an actual word."

*I'm too weak to look nor instruct you further on the proper use of the English language.*

I attempted to blow a strand of hair away from my forehead, but it stuck to my skin like it had been dipped in superglue. As a matter of fact, I'm pretty sure I'd need a steam iron to get my clothes off tonight. At least I was wearing one of my favorite broomstick skirts, which helped a bit in the heat.

Don't think it hasn't crossed my mind to utilize witchcraft to fix whatever might have happened to the power grid station. The problem with using magic was that I might actually surprise a poor lineman with a sudden restoration of power. The last thing I'd want was to electrocute someone over self-gain. You should know that my track record on past spells was a bit rocky.

*I love your ability to understate the blatantly obvious.*

"Leo, your tail only lost feeling for a tad bit that one time when I practiced creating that arthritic tea blend for Otis…and that was months ago." I opened the drawer underneath the cash register, grabbing one of numerous hair ties that I had laying around in various drawers of the tea shop. It didn't take me long to secure the damp strands away from my forehead and off the back of my neck. "And for your information, I haven't flubbed up a spell in a couple of months."

*You would go ahead and jinx yourself, wouldn't you? It doesn't matter. I'll be dead before you can cast another spell.*

"Hey, this blackout definitely wasn't because of me," I said defensively, though doubt did creep in when I thought of those who could have done such a thing. The list was rather short, but what could any of them have gained by descending Paramour Bay into complete darkness last night? "You don't think…"

*No.*

"Aunt Rowena has been visiting Mom in the city," I reminded Leo, wary that I might actually be onto something. "What if—"

*I'm not about to die talking about those...witches. I can't take this anymore, Raven. Is it possible to melt? I don't want to be a big glob of goo in the end.*

"You're not going to melt," I reassured him, though I wasn't so sure that heatstroke should be taken off the table. That was the only reasonable explanation as to why my suspicions about the blackout had veered toward witchcraft. It was most likely a blown circuit on some board that controlled some switch or something equally similar. I wasn't going to waste any more time on inviting bad karma into my life when everything had been going great. I glanced over my shoulder to look at the clock hanging on the wall. What in the world was causing Beetle to take this long? "I'm going to call—"

"Raven, Raven!"

*My BFF! He's come to save me. I'm too weak to greet him, though. Just tell him to pour the bag of ice directly on my stomach. I don't care if I get squashed, because it's better than melting in this fur coat.*

You should know before meeting Beetle that he was rather...unique. Kind of like the tea blend I'd used to make the sweet tea. The only way to describe him would be to compare him to the mad scientist from the movie *Back to the Future*. Seriously, he had the same white hair that stood up on end and similar wild blue eyes that widened every time he had a crazy idea—like dating my mother.

Beetle also had a thing for cardigans and bow ties, but even he'd had to shed the layers for a short sleeved buttoned-down dress shirt. He used to be the town's CPA before deciding to retire, thus handing over the reins to my best friend—Heidi Connolly.

It was sweet, really. Beetle had practically hired himself, not wanting to while away in his retirement. He didn't know much about tea nor was he the best salesman, but the financials of the tea shop had never been in better order.

*I'm dying of heatstroke, and you want to ramble on and on about the tea shop's accounting practices? Get your priorities straight, Raven!*

"Hi, Beetle," I greeted with a grateful smile, hopping down from the high-top stool that I kept behind the counter before walking around to take one of the large bags of ice. He'd somehow bumped into the glass door, which was slowly closing behind him. "How far did you have to drive to find these? You've been gone for hours."

"The sheriff is dead!"

The exclamation that Beetle had blurted out came with those wide eyes I was talking about, but I had to have heard him wrong. I rested the back of my hand to my forehead. Maybe Leo was right about heatstroke causing delirium.

"The sheriff is dead!" Beetle exclaimed again, dropping both unopened bags of ice in the cooler before I had a chance to recover from hearing his declaration the first time. He pressed the palms of his hands to his cheeks. He also had an odd quirk of repeating his words, which definitely brought me up short once again. Third time was a charm, right? "The sheriff is dead, Raven! I saw him lying in the middle of the street with my very own eyes!"

I finally came to an abrupt halt and stared back at Beetle in horror.

I *was* delirious.

There was no way that Sheriff Liam Drake was lying dead in the street.

It simply wasn't possible.

I would have known.

*It is possible, and I'm next. The poor fella…the good ol' sheriff probably perished from heatstroke. May his soul rest in peace. You'll find me wading in the cooler.*

"Stop it," I replied angrily, barely able to hold back my tears. This couldn't be happening. Beetle's blue eyes widened even further at my abrupt directive, fully convinced that I'd been shouting at him. Now would have been a good time to explain that no one in Paramour Bay actually knew that I was a witch, but I could barely gather my thoughts together. "I have to see for myself that Liam is okay, because you are wrong. Liam is not dead, Beetle. He just isn't."

I rushed past Beetle before he could say another word, barreling through the glass door and practically spilling onto the sidewalk. Looking frantically to my left and right, I finally spotted a crowd forming smack dab in the middle of the town's cobblestone square. My chest hurt, but it wasn't from my heart beating so fast and hard. No, it was from thinking that my time had been cut short with the one man who I truly believed was my one and only soulmate.

"Raven, you don't—"

I gathered the material of my skirt with my fingers, clutching the fabric in my hands as I quickly ran toward the commotion where the residents were hastily creating a circle. I ignored the fact that Beetle was calling my name from behind me, because there was no way I could stop until I saw with my own very eyes that the man I loved was alive and well. He couldn't have been taken away from me too soon. He just couldn't have. There had to be some mistake.

"Move," I pleaded with Albert and Eugene, the two older

gentlemen who always played chess over at Monty's hardware store. I shouldered past them with a mumbled apology, dodging around Desmond Barnes who happened to own the malt store next to my tea shop. "Please, let me get by."

I wasn't even sure how I got the words out around my constricted throat without breaking down, but I couldn't accept what Beetle had blurted out so callously without definitive proof.

"I need to—"

I stopped short after practically shoving Bree Stonehedge to the side when I finally set my frantic gaze on Liam—who just happened to be standing across from me and the bakery shop owner.

*Would you look at that? The good ol' sheriff is alive and well.*

"Isn't it just horrible?" Bree muttered, seemingly having ignored the fact that I'd nearly knocked her down. "That poor man. Do you think he had a heart attack?"

"Maybe heatstroke," Paula answered while holding up a hand to keep the sun out of her eyes. She was one of the waitresses at the diner across the street. "Terrible thing, this."

*See? I told you that I was showing signs of heatstroke. By the way, my symptoms are worse now that I'm standing on this boiling asphalt. My paws might actually be smoking.*

Liam recognized right away that I was part of the group of gawkers whom he was trying to disband, and he lowered his brow in concern by what must have been pure panic written across my perspiring features. He continued to wave for everyone to back away from the dead body while silently asking if I was okay.

Honestly, it was a wonder that I hadn't joined the man lying dead at my feet.

*I've already got that spot reserved. Do you think they would mind if I stood on the body? I mean, my paws are really burning.*

I could only nod jerkily in answer to Liam's unspoken inquiry, hoping that he didn't think I was having some sort of seizure. To cover up the fact that I was still trying to compose myself and to make sure that Leo's paws weren't being damaged, I bent my knees and hoisted Leo into my arms. No easy feat, but it afforded me the ability to take a few more seconds for my body to catch up with what my sight was signaling to my brain—the sheriff whom Beetle had been referring to wasn't Liam.

Instead, a tall man wearing a sheriff's uniform and who appeared to be in his fifties was lying dead in the middle of the cobblestone square. I'd never seen him before in my life. I wouldn't wish death on my worst enemy, but I couldn't deny that relief coursed through my veins upon discovering that Liam was alive and well.

*I already said that. Listen, I will have you know that I left my battery-operated fan, bowl of water, and a bag of ice to come out here in this stifling heat and blazing sun just to comfort you. You holding me against your sweaty body is going to have both of us lying next to that dead sheriff at our feet.*

"What happened?" I asked softly to anyone who would listen.

*I can't breathe...that's what happening.*

You should know that Leo had the ability to materialize and disappear in the blink of an eye. No one else could hear him besides witches and warlocks, and absolutely no one else knew of his special ability to become invisible. With that said, I hadn't wanted him to completely vanish, leaving behind a puff of orange and black strands.

Liam had enough on his hands with a dead body lying in the

middle of the town square. I didn't want to make things worse by revealing my secret in such a spectacular way. There were quite a few things I had yet to disclose to him.

*Let's keep it that way, shall we? We'll just call it my dying wish.*

"Monty was getting into his car, hoping to get some relief using the air conditioning in his vehicle by driving around town when he saw this man just lying in the middle of the road," Paula explained, her lips turning down in sorrow. "Monty yelled for help, and thankfully Liam was exiting the police station. It was too late, though. Liam already called that handsome state police detective who Heidi has been dating."

*Great. Now I have to die with seeing my sweet Heidi fawn all over that oaf of a detective. He couldn't find his rear end with both hands. What did I do to deserve such a horrifying death?*

Liam wouldn't have called Jack Swanson if there wasn't some sort of sign of foul play. Paramour Bay was a one-sheriff town. Anything more than jaywalking or settling neighborly disputes was usually ferreted out to the state police. As for the dead sheriff, he wasn't from around here.

I didn't want to cause Leo any more stress than he was already under with the blackout and oppressing heat, but he could also read every thought that crossed my mind. It was impossible to keep him from knowing that the palm of my right hand began to tingle with energy.

*It's nothing more than the heat, Raven. It could very well be me. My beloved Heidi is always telling my how hot I am as a tomcat. Let's head back to the tea shop, shall we? There's two bags of ice, and one of them has my name written all over it. You can use the other bag to stick your hand in, because it's too darn hot to get involved in another mystery right now. Raven, are you even listening to me?*

No amount of distractions from Leo was going to stop the

energy from coiling in my palm, which was usually a sign that danger was somewhere near.

*I can still try, so let's do this one more time. Turn around, force your legs to walk toward the tea shop where those heavenly ice bags await us, and we can forget this ever happened. Imagine a nice cool glass of your iced tea. It's simple, really.*

The sound of a police siren could be heard in the distance.

*I don't hear anything. Oh, Raven. I think you're having symptoms of heatstroke. We really should head back to the tea shop before you get us entangled in all of this.*

We'd all shuffled back about twenty feet to give Liam the ability to clear the area for the officers arriving on the scene, who would investigate to make sure this sheriff's death had been of natural causes.

Unfortunately, given that a dead body of a sheriff was lying dead in the middle of the town's cobblestone square with an item by his side that was very much out of place, I was pretty sure there was a valid reason that the palm of my hand had begun to harness energy.

*You're just hallucinating. I don't see a thing.*

The item in question was a broomstick.

*I'm already dying of heatstroke. Can't we just let the good ol' sheriff and that oaf of a detective take the first crack at this case? Really, Raven, there's no need to investigate every mystery that crosses our path. We aren't in the law enforcement business.*

I studied the object in question a little more closely, and it wasn't the everyday broom that one could buy at a local store nowadays. No, the broomstick lying next to the dead body of the sheriff was actually that—one of those antique broomsticks made from birch twigs with a chestnut handle.

*My asthma finally kicked in. Are you happy now? This is it,*

*Raven. I've used up my nine lives, so it's best to get me back to the tea shop. Just lay my body on that bag of ice so that I can die in peace.*

No one was dying on my watch.

*You realize that we're standing over a dead guy, right?*

A sheriff, from whom I assume was from a neighboring town, might possibly have been murdered. The palm of my right hand wouldn't be hotter than my already overheated body if that wasn't the case, and the old-fashioned broomstick was pointing in only one direction as to what could have been the cause— witchcraft.

*You couldn't have just let me die in peace, could you? That would have been too easy, huh?*

# Chapter Two

"ARE YOU CERTAIN the sheriff was murdered?" Heidi whispered, glancing over her shoulder to make sure that Beetle wasn't within earshot. The Chinese handmade folding fan she held in her fingers never stopped moving in her attempt to keep cool. "I mean, we're in the middle of a heatwave. The man might simply have dropped dead from heatstroke."

*Heidi gets me. If you remember correctly, that is exactly what I said.*

Leo's sigh of contentment garnered an annoyed sideways glance from me. He had literally planted himself on top of one of the bags of ice with all four pudgy paws dangling down the sides, and Beetle hadn't had the heart to move him and empty the bag into the cooler.

*My BFF gets me, too. They both treat me like I'm exactly who I am. I'm not sure what your problem is, Raven. You should get with the program. You'd think I hung around after your grandmother's death just to annoy you.*

"I suspect because neither one of them lives every day and night with you inside of their head," I practically hissed at him, unable to keep my mouth shut any longer. Beetle was standing just outside the glass door of the tea shop, shading his eyes with his right hand as he continued to monitor the progress of the crime scene. He'd been keeping us informed with each step of the process, and it seemed the coroner was ready to place the sheriff into a body bag. "Heidi, I'm telling you that it felt like my hand was on fire. I don't think that the sheriff's death had anything remotely to do with natural causes."

My best friend had recently moved to Paramour Bay from New York City. She'd bought her first house three months ago, signed the papers to take over Beetle's old accounting firm with his clientele, and she was the one person I called when I needed personal advice. The bonus in this situation was that Heidi knew all about me, my witchcraft, and the fact that there were other creatures and critters of the supernatural realm who walked among us.

*Only one of the many rules you've broken over the last ten months. I have a color-coded list somewhere, but not even the Yellowstone Supervolcano exploding could get me to move off this bag of heaven.*

"Have you called Rye?" Heidi asked, using her free hand to lift her blonde curls from her neck. I intuitively opened the drawer where I had a ton of hair ties stashed, handing one over to her. "Maybe he sensed a ripple in the force, too?"

*You can save yourself a phone call. The resident warlock left for Windsor until the blackout is over. I'd say he chose the smart path, but I'd rather melt into a pile of orange and black goo before I went to stay with Rowena. Also, could you tell Heidi this isn't* Star Wars, *although I do bear a striking resemblance to Chewy.*

For once today, Leo and I agreed on something. I mean, the Rowena part…not the Chewy part.

Aunt Rowena was technically my great aunt. She was part of the reason my Nan had separated from the coven. She'd been Nan's sister, and the two never did manage to resolve their issues before my grandmother's untimely passing. The only reason

Aunt Rowena was hovering on the sidelines of my life was due to a war that she was cultivating between two factions of the coven—a coven that Nan had been excommunicated from, and one that I wanted nothing to do with. The fierce battle ahead was the only reason Aunt Rowena was cozying up to my mother, but I had faith that Mom was too smart to fall for any horse malarkey our aunt came up with in the meantime.

*That's debatable. Your mother isn't the sharpest Crayola in the box.*

"Rye is up in Windsor with Aunt Rowena," I reiterated to Heidi, who was used to me having side conversations with Leo. She'd set down her fan to gather up her blonde curls and secure them in a messy bun on top of her head. "He probably doesn't even know what happened here yet."

*Let's keep it that way. I can only deal with one accident-prone witch or warlock at a time. You two are like a traffic accident. I do my best to avoid the multi-car pileups.*

"Well, don't do anything crazy," Heidi advised me, which was laughable. She was usually the first one to lead the charge into getting us both in trouble with her spontaneous ways. "Liam always keeps you in the loop, so you can ask him about the details of what happened today when he stops by later."

I didn't even want to think back to my reaction when Beetle had come charging into the tea shop claiming that the sheriff was dead. He'd apologized profusely when I'd finally walked back to the storefront with Leo in tow. Beetle had tried to say something once he realized his mistake, but by that time I was running out the door. My arms were still shaking from all that weight I had been carrying, but at least Leo was content for the moment.

*Not quite. I'll know contentment when you tell me that you'll leave the sheriff's death to the proper authorities. Speaking of sheriffs, yours is like one of those fruit flies. He just keeps appearing out of nowhere and floating around until all I want to do is swat him.*

Leo absolutely hated the fact that I was dating anyone, but especially a regular human. Being new to witchcraft, it took a lot of my time to learn the casting of spells and the limitations of my abilities as an elemental witch. He was afraid I'd slip and blurt out all my secrets, like I'd intentionally done with Heidi.

*Considering the one main rule of the coven was that no human should be made aware of the supernatural realm, it's a good thing your family was already excommunicated. I'm still not convinced the council isn't going to show up on our doorstep to turn us all into toads. Green is not my color. And you already know I detest fruit flies.*

"Well, the crowd has dispersed and the visiting sheriff's body has been loaded into a body bag," Beetle advised us, having stepped back over the threshold of the shop. He fished out a handkerchief from the small pocket of his short-sleeved dress shirt before using it to dab the perspiration from his brow. "This bag of ice is melting at a fast pace, my dear Raven. A very fast pace. It's no wonder that all the residents are flocking to the hotels over in New Haven. Even Gertie's 40k generator over at the inn is struggling to keep the lower level cool enough for her guests to be comfortable during the heat of the day."

"I ran into Eugene and Albert on my way over here," Heidi shared, still fanning herself while I chomped on a piece of ice. "They saw most of the inn's guests leave right before all the excitement. I've closed up my office, and I'm seriously contemplating driving into New Haven myself if the electric company can't get the power restored by tonight. I need to get one of those generators for my place. They have ones now that kick on automatically when the power goes out."

*Tell Heidi I'm going with her. She might have to carry me to her brand-new car, though. I don't think I have the strength to remove myself from this bag.*

"Beetle, I'm going to close up the shop." I wrapped my hand around the tea cup I was using to hold my ice. I'd given up keeping the sweet tea cold, and no one wanted to consume a hot beverage when the outside temperature was closing in on a hundred degrees Fahrenheit. Well, except me…but I could drink coffee under any circumstances. The lack of my favorite beverage wasn't doing anything for my current mood. I needed to get one of those old-fashioned coffee percolators one could use over an actual burner. I'd have to add it to my list of inventory for the shop. "Why don't you drive into the city to see my mother? I'm sure she'll be thrilled to have an impromptu visit from you, and this way you can get a reprieve from this heat."

*Did you just…*

Yes, I'd just suggested that Beetle go see my mother. It was better than having him here and accidentally overhearing me discuss the fact that I think witchcraft might be the main cause for a sheriff who dropped dead in the town's cobblestone square.

*Heatstroke. That's the only viable reason you would suggest such a thing. Tell Heidi we need to take a detour to the hospital. I can't have you walking about spouting such blubber.*

I'm pretty sure that my reasons were vastly different from Leo's objections as to why my mother shouldn't be dating my part-time employee. Leo was just worried it would affect his special treats of catnip that Beetle ordered as a specialty from some farm in Honduras. I was more worried that Beetle would get his heart broken into a million itsy-bitsy pieces.

Trust me, you'd understand my concern if you knew my mother the way I did.

"What a grand idea, Raven!" Beetle exclaimed in excitement, shoving his handkerchief back into his shirt pocket before giving Heidi and I a small bow of appreciation. "Grand idea! You two ladies try to stay cool and have a wonderful afternoon. I'll just be on my way then!"

Beetle quickly turned on the heels of his dress shoes with a whistle and marched across the threshold of the opened glass door. I immediately reached for an ice cube and dropped it down my shirt, catching my breath when the cold square landed inside my bra. I closed my eyes as the cool respite was almost instantaneous.

"Leo, one word about where I put that ice cube, and I'll take away that entire bag of ice that you're wasting for your own pleasure," I warned, wondering if I shouldn't join Heidi for a girl's night at some swanky hotel that had air conditioning, movie channels, and room service. There was only so much a woman could take without losing her mind. "How long are you going to give the electric company to fix the power before you head out of town?"

The chime of Heidi's cell phone began to sound, cutting off her answer. I didn't even have to ask who was calling as a wide smile began to grace her lips. Well, there went the girl's night out.

*Sickening, is what it is. That oaf of a detective has her bamboo-zled. Raven, can you come here and flip me over?*

Giving Heidi some privacy, I hopped off my stool and grabbed my tea cup full of ice. To give you an indication of just how hot it was in Paramour Bay, the ice cube in my bra had already melted. There was no doubt that a water stain would be making itself known through the material of my shirt, but I was already sticky with perspiration. No one would know the difference.

*Hey, where are you going? Give a cat a flip, why don't you?*

"Leo, the bag is almost nothing but water." I walked closer to the opened glass door of the tea shop, noticing that Eileen was waving to someone through the police station's window. I searched the sidewalk for her target. "I'll call the electric company soon and try to get another ETA on when they think the electricity will be turned back on. I didn't live here last summer, but I've never heard of Paramour Bay having a literal blackout for more than a few hours, let alone an entire day."

*My ice melted? I thought this felt like a waterbed. Look, Raven. I can float.*

Sure enough, a quick glance over my shoulder showed that Leo was attempting to wobble back and forth. His weight prevented him from doing so gracefully, but it was still cute to see that he was having a bit of fun and not being obsessed with the fact that we might just have another murder mystery to solve.

*You know how to rain on a parade, don't you?*

"Stop being so cranky," I scolded, all the while realizing that I'd been quite short-tempered, too. "I'm hot, too. We all are."

I didn't wait for one of Leo's snarky comments, but I'm pretty sure he mentioned something about moving to Alaska and growing catnip. Walking across the metal plate on the threshold, I made sure to stay underneath the shade of the small awning in front of the shop. There wasn't even the slightest breeze to give me a bit of respite from the heat, and the gold tassels were hanging limp from the canopy above. I'm surprised the hand-painted name of *Tea, Leaves, & Eves* hadn't melted from the plate glass window.

I rested the porcelain tea cup against my cheek as I watched Liam talking with Monty across the street. Liam was who Eileen had been trying to gain attention from, but he was too busy jotting something down in his notepad to notice. Knowing that Jack probably wasn't far away, I scanned the sidewalks and street for any sign of the detective. I finally spotted him sitting in the driver's side seat of his unmarked police car with his cell phone to his ear. He lifted his fingers from the steering wheel when he saw me looking his way, and I returned his kind gesture.

It was rather odd that the town had gone about its usual routine after having found a dead body in the middle of the town's square. Then again, it wasn't like any of them could do anything to change what had happened. It appeared to be an accident. It was just offbeat to know that someone's life could be snuffed out by supernatural means and the regular world kept turning without even the slightest pause.

Nan had suffered a heart attack on her daily walk over ten months ago, dropping dead almost in the exact same spot. Is that why I thought there was something odd with the sheriff's death or was it the telltale broom?

Was I projecting my suspicion of witchcraft onto a natural human death merely because he'd died in the same manner? Or was it witchcraft, after all?

For all I knew, there was a perfectly reasonable explanation as to why there was that specific type of broomstick lying next to the body of a dead man. It might not have anything to do with witchcraft, but that object was often used in hexes. After all, we did have an antique store here in town and for some odd reason humans thought those types of brooms were adorable. How far of a stretch was it to believe that the sheriff collected such odd pieces to decorate his home?

"Change of plans. I'm heading back into the city with Jack," Heidi said, startling me out of my reverie as she suddenly appeared in the doorway. She continued to flick her wrist, waving the fan in front of her face as she joined me underneath the shade of the awning. "Do you and Leo want to follow us? I'm sure he wouldn't mind it if you crashed on his couch for a night. This place is beginning to look more and more like a ghost town every second that ticks by without electricity."

*I'd rather die from heatstroke than set one paw in that oaf's apartment!*

Leo must have still been splayed out on the bag of ice that had all but turned to water, because his voice sounded as if he were still inside the shop. I'm glad he was in agreement with staying in Paramour Bay, though. We had some things to sort out before we could head out of town.

Liam chose that moment to turn away from Monty in order to head back to the station. The fact that he immediately glanced over at me warmed my heart, and I lifted my tea cup in recognition. He gave me a half smile and held up all five fingers, alerting me to the fact that he'd be over to visit in another five minutes.

*I'm going to need to eat the rest of my catnip if I'm going to handle a visit from the good ol' sheriff. Now that I've had time to ponder our situation, maybe we should take a ride out to the power grid station. If we can get someone to tell us what happened, then I formally tender my vote for taking the chance of you flubbing up a spell to try and fix it. I mean, how much worse can it get? Broken is broken.*

An ice cube almost lodged in my throat that Leo had tempted fate, because he was constantly lecturing me about jinxing our good streaks. We'd had many conversations over this very subject.

*Desperate times calls for desperate measures.*

"I appreciate the offer, Heidi. I really do, but I think I'm going to stay behind to make sure we don't have another murder on our hands as a result of…" I wiggled the fingers on my left hand to imitate casting magic. "I also don't want to leave the shop for that long. I read somewhere that heatwaves like this can cause people to do crazy things. Add in the fact that we have no power, and I really want to be close by in case anything else happens."

*Give this catnip ten minutes to kick in, and I'll be ready to take a ride in that death contraption you call a car. The air conditioning isn't the best, but it's better than nothing, so that's a huge plus.*

"I'm not going anywhere until I talk to Liam and find out what happened to that sheriff," I said to Leo after having said goodbye to Heidi. She was already halfway across the street to Jack, who'd opened his car door to greet her. "Maybe it's a good thing Heidi is going into the city, just in case we try a spell and somehow set a match to the whole town."

*Who is this* we *you speak of? You must have a mouse in your pocket.*

"You're my partner in crime," I replied with a smile as I pressed the cold tea cup to my chest after turning around to poke my head back in the shop's entrance. There were only a few ice chips left. "You can't fool me, Leo. You wouldn't have it any other way."

"Am I being replaced by the cat?"

Suddenly, two arms came around my waist and brought me back against a hard chest. I didn't mind the additional body heat, nor did I mind the small kiss that had been gently pressed to the back of my neck.

"Don't you know that you're irreplaceable?" I teased, turning around to face Liam.

*I feel a hairball at the back of my throat.*

Liam's brow was damp with perspiration, and he'd swapped out his usual khaki buttoned-down dress shirt that was his staple when on shift. In its place was a light-colored short-sleeved shirt with a small V in the front. He had been smiling, but it gradually faded as he studied my expression.

"What happened earlier? You had me worried when you almost shoved Bree to the ground out there."

"You saw that, huh?" I asked, wishing I'd been a little more discreet. In my defense, I'd been in the throes of a panic attack. "It's going to sound foolish, but Beetle came into the tea shop and declared that the sheriff was dead."

I didn't have to wait long before Liam comprehended how the scene must have unfolded earlier. A bright smile began to curl on his lips, and I had a feeling I wouldn't be living this moment down anytime soon.

*Heatstroke would be preferable than listening to this sappy stuff.*

"You thought I'd died?"

I pushed hard against Liam's chest, not finding any humor in this situation. His rich laughter eventually faded, and he gave me the most reassuring smile I'd ever seen.

"I'm not that easy to get rid of, Raven."

*Now who's tempting fate?*

Leo had definitely just hacked up a hairball. In spite of that, a shiver of unease traveled through my spine, but not for the reasons you might think.

You see, Liam had been dropping these one-liners over the last couple of months that made me believe he knew I was keeping a secret from him. There had even been a few references that caused me to think he was seriously talking about the supernatural.

*I'm pretty sure delusions and hallucinations are symptoms of heatstroke. Listen, you know I wouldn't offer this to just anyone...but come lay on this formerly cold bag of ice that is now mildly cool water.*

"That's good to know," I replied with a small smile, hoping to cover up my suspicions. It was best to make sure that my secret didn't get revealed by a sheriff who been found dead with an unusual broomstick by his side. "What happened to that poor man? Did he have a heart attack?"

*Good diversion, Raven. Well done. You keep him occupied from asking too many questions, confirm that the sheriff's death was from natural causes, and then we can go for a ride in that deathtrap you call a vehicle.*

The only reason that Leo was referring to my beat-up old Corolla as a death contraption was to cover up the fact that he was to blame for my back bumper falling off after he'd jumped on top of it the other day.

*I have no idea what you're talking about. I landed as light as a feather.*

"We're not sure," Liam replied with a grimace, motioning for me to step back underneath the awning. He joined me in the shade, using the ledge of the window to lean against as he continued to monitor the comings and goings of those who were still in town. "The sheriff was from a small town located between here and New Haven. Jack sent an officer to touch base with the man's family and his deputy to inform them of his death, but we won't know the official cause until after the autopsy."

*Heatstroke is no laughing matter.*

"Did you know him?" I asked, joining Liam against the small ledge. I offered him one of my ice chips in sympathy. "Personally, or professionally?"

"I met him briefly at a meeting once when some vandals were hitting small towns a while back." Liam took one of the three ice chips left and plopped it into his mouth. "Pat O'Leary was his name, and he seemed like a decent enough man."

*May he rest in peace.*

"You seem concerned about something." I shifted the cup in my hands so that I was only touching the handle. I didn't want my body heat melting the last two ice chips. "I also don't think you would have called in Jack had you thought it was from natural causes."

*You just had to go there, didn't you, Raven?*

I held my breath for Liam's answer, though that wasn't the wisest thing to do when I was already about to pass out from the heat. I took one of the remaining two ice chips and held it against the back of my neck.

*That's it. I'm putting both my paws down. We're not playing amateur sleuths again until the power comes back on.*

"Sheriff O'Leary had a note in his hand," Liam revealed, his dark gaze meeting mine. There was a mixture of concern and unease in those brown eyes of his, and a wave of anxiety hit me in the stomach. "It was a list of herbal poisons, Raven."

*I'm going on strike. Did you hear that, Raven? No sleuthing until we have the ability to work from the comfort of central air conditioning.*

"You think Sheriff O'Leary was poisoned? I don't understand," I said, my mind racing in several different directions. Thankfully, not one of them led to witchcraft. Unfortunately, the man had still lost his life by someone's hand. "If the sheriff thought he'd ingested something that could kill him, why wouldn't he have gone to the hospital?"

"Exactly," Liam replied grimly. He lifted a hand, causing me to look and see who had caught his attention. Eileen was motioning for Liam to come back to the station, her bright t-shirt of daffodils hard to miss. "There was something else."

*No, there wasn't something else. The good ol' sheriff does like to exaggerate at times, doesn't he? Hey, Raven. You should really come in here and lay on this bag. The water is still somewhat temperate.*

Leo was saying anything and everything to distract me from what Liam was about to say, but I wasn't about to be deterred when I was so close to getting to the truth.

*You make my life so difficult at times.*

"The sheriff went into the antique store to ask about a very strange item from the 1800s," Liam revealed, pushing away from the windowsill ledge. He needed to go see what Eileen needed, which was most likely about the case. Unfortunately, the palm of my hand began to tingle. Liam was about to reveal something that could very well have this case threaten the one secret I couldn't allow to be revealed to the residents of this town. "Turns out, the object in question was a broomstick with a rather strange curse associated with it…whoever has it in their possession dies a horrible death."

*Raven, tell me that you didn't touch that hexed broomstick.*

# Chapter Three

"LEO, YOU'RE GETTING fur all over my car," I complained, flipping my turn signal on to indicate that I was pulling into the substation of the local electric company. There was no one behind me nor had there been all the way out on this edge of town, but it was an ingrained habit of driving. "I'm rethinking this case. Maybe I should have asked Heidi to stay behind to help."

Leo was leaning against the far vent, his whiskers pressed into the slats as the cool air did its best to keep up with the oppressive heat. My vehicle was pretty old, but she was still running like a charm. Granted, the air conditioning could have been slightly cooler, but neither one of us was going to whine about it when we were better off inside the car than the tea shop that currently acted like a furnace.

*I'm here with you, aren't I? I hate when you infer I'm nothing more than chopped liver. I don't trust anyone who says they like that nasty stuff.*

"You know how much I appreciate your company." I figured it was better to butter Leo up in case this latest murder mystery did turn out to have supernatural elements included with it. It didn't take long to pull parallel to the chain link fence. "Uh-oh. We have a problem."

I quickly stepped on the gas, inadvertently causing Leo to fly back against the passenger side seat. He disappeared in a blink, only to reappear sitting on his tail and scrambling to look dignified.

*What is wrong with you? Give a cat some kind of warning next time, would you? I swear, you complain about claw marks in virtually everything I touch, and then you go and pull shenanigans like that.*

"Sorry," I muttered, sparing a glance in my rearview mirror. I'm not sure why I thought that the substation would be void of any people, but there were two trucks parked in front while a handful of employees were looking over the equipment. "Shoot. We're going to have to find something else connected to the substation to utilize the spell you came up with."

Leo had managed to shift his rather heavy frame until he was back in front of the vent. This time he had a firm grip. I'd pulled the passenger seat as close as I could to the dashboard, allowing him easier access to the vents. Had Leo been an ordinary housecat, I never would have been so irresponsible. A familiar had the ability to disappear and reappear in the blink of an eye.

*There's a pull off up ahead. We can—*

Leo's gasp had me jerking the steering wheel, fully believing something was about to run across the street in front of us.

*Skippy! My archnemesis! Pull over, Raven. Pull over right now!*

"Leo, you almost gave me a heart attack," I exclaimed, wincing when I realized it was possible the sheriff had still died in such a horrible manner. "It's too hot for you to chase Skippy all over town."

With that said, I did pull over onto the left-hand side of the road. We were around a quarter mile outside of town, but it was foolish to keep driving when there was no place for me to cast a spell. At least, not one that I could think of off the top of my

Leo literally disappeared from the front passenger seat, leaving me to pull the vehicle to a stop and wait for him. It was far too hot for him to be using magic the way he was, and it was only a matter of time before he needed to be hydrated.

I reached for a bottle of warm water that I'd taken from the cooler at the tea shop, wishing it was still cold. Even I knew that drinking lots of water in this type of heat was a necessity.

Having done a one-hundred-and-eighty-degree turn, the front part of my beat-up old Corolla was now facing town. As I was putting the white cap back onto the water bottle, I saw movement out of my peripheral vision.

Sure enough, Skippy had gone running into the foliage. I didn't catch hide nor hair of Leo, but then again, he'd left enough fur flying around the interior of my car. It was a wonder I could even breathe.

"Come on, Leo," I muttered, tapping my thumb on the steering wheel.

Sitting in a car under the blazing sun wasn't such a good idea, and I could literally feel the heat seeping into the console in front of me. I'd give Leo only a few more minutes before I went to look for him.

I couldn't stop my thoughts from turning to what Liam had said about the broomstick...a cursed broomstick. Leo had said such things could happen, and I'd certainly witnessed enough supernatural events to believe it could happen.

But what in the world was a sheriff doing with an antique cursed broomstick and a list of herbal poisons clutched in his hand at the time of his death?

At least I had the sheriff's name. It would make it easier to investigate his death in order to figure out if it was a result of a curse or maybe due to some type of black magic. There was still a chance Sheriff O'Leary's death had been nothing more than a heart attack induced by the stress of the heat.

I'd feel even more comfortable with the latter supposition if I could prove that this blackout wasn't initiated by witchcraft.

*Drive!*

I'll admit it.

I screamed like a banshee.

Leo had suddenly materialized next to me, looking a little worse for wear…which was saying quite a lot. I covered my chest with a trembling hand, trying to even out my breathing so that I didn't hyperventilate.

It was a serious probability, considering the effect this heat-wave was having on my body.

*Wow. You're a horrible getaway driver.*

"Leo, don't do that," I scolded, resting my head back against the headrest. "What did you do?"

*I found the reason for the power outage, and you need to go tell those men back at the substation so we can get our air conditioning back on the way it should be.*

"Wait, so the blackout wasn't due to magic?"

*Have I ever steered you wrong? Wait. Don't answer that. I don't remember, and I'm still too hot to put strain on what brain cells I have left after that necromancy spell. Get us to that substation so those wonderful workers can fix this horrible situation.*

Relief washed over me, although it wasn't enough to cool my body temperature. I pressed on the gas pedal, not wanting to waste any more time, either.

"What did you find in those woods?" I asked, not having to drive far to reach our destination. This time, I flipped my turn signal and actually maneuvered my car next to one of the utility trucks. "What caused the blackout?"

*Who do you think? Skippy, that hairy rat and his tribe of ninja squirrels, that's who! He and his friends were having some secret meeting in one of the trees, probably about me. Anyway, the tree was rotted and a huge branch ended up on a ton of wires. I can't believe that gang of ninja squirrels didn't end up electrocuted, leaving all their skeletons for me to find.*

The ongoing annual battle between Leo and Skippy had been running on for years. I'm pretty sure that Leo took it a bit more seriously than Skippy, but I wasn't going to look a gift horse in the mouth.

*We've got a month or two left before those ninja squirrels start to gather what nuts are left on the ground for the upcoming winter. They'll plan an attack on me next month...I just know it! Wait just a darn acorn...do you think Skippy and his band of warriors did this on purpose to drive me out of town?*

"No," I answered fast and rather bluntly, not wanting Leo to take the next few days planning out another massive attack on the town's squirrel population. "Skippy couldn't have planned for the tree to fall on the wires or whatever equipment it hit next to the station."

I'd worked out in my mind the direction that Skippy had taken when he'd disappeared into the foliage. Whatever tree Leo was talking about had to be close to the back end of the substation. That would explain why so many workers were currently searching for damage at the local substation.

*I'm not so sure about that, Raven. I'm almost certain I caught sight of a beaver down by the stream. What if Skippy made a backend deal and turned the toothy critter against me?*

"Stop seeing conspiracies where there aren't any," I whispered, stopping my car and waving toward one of the workers through the front windshield. The man began to walk across the gravel, but it was apparent he wasn't happy about being summoned by one of the local residents. I had a feeling that I wasn't the only one to stop to talk to them about the blackout, but what he didn't know was that I might be able to shed some light on the problem. "Here goes nothing."

*Do you think the library has a database of all the wildlife in and around Paramour Bay? You should suggest that to Harry. A librarian such as himself should always keep good records for these very reasons.*

I rolled down my window and gave the employee a big smile, hoping to butter him up before he tried to send me on my way. *Just so you are reassured about me sounding like a lunatic in front of Harry, I had no intention of telling Harry that he should catalog the wildlife in and around town.*

*I'm pretty sure I've already told you today that you make my life very difficult. And I'd like to remind you that you're the one who was tossing conspiracies around regarding the blackout being caused by witchcraft. I blame the heat.*

"Hi, there," I exclaimed brightly, motioning over my shoulder at Leo. "I had to go looking for my cat back in the woods, and I think I know what might have happened to cause the blackout."

*You're not taking me seriously about this squirrel apocalypse. If Skippy is recruiting beavers, this changes the whole board game.*

"Our systems test is showing that there is a short on the step-down transformer at this station. What did you see, ma'am?"

"There was a tree lying on top of some big metal thing back there," I explained, pointing in the direction where Leo had gone in chase of Skippy. "I didn't get too close, because I wasn't sure if there were any wires down on the ground. But it looked like there was pretty extensive damage done to whatever it is you would call one of those large metal devices."

The worker hit the top of my vehicle in appreciation, taking off at a brisk pace in order to inform the others of what could possibly be the cause of their headaches. I waited a moment longer to make sure they began to walk in the right direction before settling back in my seat with satisfaction for a job well done.

*What metal device?*

Oh, that wasn't good. Not to get off topic, but that necromancy spell that Nan had cast to prevent Leo from crossing over into the afterlife had really affected his memory. The majority of the time it was short-term memory, but there had been instances where his memory loss had gone further back over the years.

"The metal thingy that the tree fell on," I explained, pressing down on the accelerator with one of my favorite black flats. I usually preferred my high-top black boots, but I'd stored them away until the cooler weather arrived…which currently felt like it would never come. "Remember chasing Skippy through the woods?"

I'd maneuvered my car onto the road into town, but the cool air that we'd had trapped inside had escaped the second I'd rolled down my window to talk with one of the linemen. It was highly doubtful that we'd get the interior cooled off before arriving back at the tea shop. Leo had taken back his position and was leaning his cheek against the open vent, and I didn't blame him.

*Skippy? I should have known that hairy rat was involved. Whatever. I'm too overheated now to care. You should have asked how long it would take for them to fix this horrible situation.*

"I'm just glad that magic had nothing to do with the blackout," I shared with relief, especially now that it shouldn't be too much longer before we were basking in the central air conditioning. "That only leaves—"

*Don't ruin my moment.*

"Leo, we can't ignore the fact that—"

*We can ignore whatever we like, because we're not officially badge holders in this tiny village. The good ol' sheriff holds that honor, and he's already handed the case off to that oaf of a detective with the state police. Do you know what the chances are of that broomstick being cursed for real?*

"Thirty-eight percent."

Leo blinked, his left eye bulging a little more as he realized that my statistics were pretty darn accurate. In fact, I was pretty proud of myself, given that math hadn't been my best subject in school.

*Exactly. So…we're in agreement to let this case go, right?*

"Nope," I quipped, thinking it might be best to head straight to the cottage on the other side of town. A cold shower was sounding better and better. Afterward, the power might be restored, and we could do some research on the computer in comfort. "I hate to break this to you, Leo, but we have a genuine murder mystery to solve."

*Not if I succumb to heatstroke first.*

# Chapter Four

*H*OW IS IT *even possible that the giant grey Crayola hasn't melted by now?*

"How are you holding up, Ted?" I asked, feeling very refreshed after having taken a cold shower. Unfortunately, the electricity hadn't come back on just yet. Skippy and his friends probably had no idea the extent of damage they'd wreaked on Paramour Bay. "Come on in. I was hoping you'd stop by this evening. I have some questions about broomsticks, curses, and death."

*Go figure. A wax golem, and he doesn't even melt in the middle of a heatwave. Your grandmother must have added something to her enchantment to provide for this eventuality. This only goes to show you that she favored this lump of wax more, or else she would have shown a little more care in preparing for my disposition rather than adding six pounds to my haunches.*

Six pounds? More like sixteen, but I wasn't going to touch that number with a ten-foot pole.

*Now would be a good time for you to introduce Ted. He's not the run of the mill supernatural creature that goes bump in the night, you know.*

True, so I'll make this one quick.

You see, when Nan had been excommunicated from the coven, she'd chosen to spend the rest of her mortal existence in

Paramour Bay. She'd open the tea shop, sold holistic blends, and raised my mother in this very special out-of-the-way town. Unfortunately, my mother left and moved to the city in her early twenties. Bottom line was that Nan had needed a bit of extra help around the old witchy abode, and I'm sure the additional company wasn't so bad either.

*Really? Ted isn't the most animated of conversationalists, and he's literally Lurch from* The Addams Family.

Leo wasn't exaggerating.

Ted used to be one of the wax figures on display at the wax museum. The somewhat creepy place was located to the left immediately upon entering the town limits. It was an odd attraction to be set in such an area, but who was I to question other people's business decisions?

Anyway, just visualize a wax figure of Lurch from *The Addams Family.*

Yep, that's Ted—lanky build, yellowish-blond hair, and at least six feet, six inches tall. He had these crooked teeth with some very noticeable chips, an odd fascination for a mannequin at a boutique shop in town, and I'd only ever seen him wear suits that were cut in the style of the late 1800s. He was always a gentleman through and through.

*Don't forget to mention that wax boy plays poker on the weekends with a grim reaper disguised as the groundskeeper over at the cemetery. I still haven't gotten my invite.*

"Good evening, Ms. Raven."

Ted closed the front door behind him as I made my way back to the couch.

"The power should be restored soon, thanks to Leo and his detective skills," I shared, finally able to give credit where credit was due. "He was chasing after Skippy and found a large tree had fallen on a vital part of the substation."

"Very nicely done, Mr. Leo."

*At least someone treats me with the respect I deserve.*

It was still stifling hot inside the cottage, but I'd opened all the windows hoping the electricity would roar to life sometime soon. The slightest breeze was finally coming in off the bay and filled the house with the scent of lilacs, but it hardly did a thing to lower the inside temperature.

"May I sit?"

I'd already sunk into the couch and had my laptop balancing on my knees when Ted had made his strange request.

He never sat.

Never.

Leo was currently splayed out in front of a small battery-powered fan on top of the hand-carved coffee table that served as both a magical temple for all the enchanted items I kept in its secret drawers and a gorgeous centerpiece for the one-story cottage. There was a bedroom loft which could be reached by a beautiful spiral staircase, but I'd have to explain the layout later.

Right now, I wasn't so sure that those symptoms of heatstroke Leo had been spouting on about all day hadn't finally emerged.

*That might be it, you know. We might have just hallucinated this entire day, and there's no dead body linked to a cursed broomstick. What are the chances I could convince you of that?*

"You want to sit down?" I asked Ted, tilting my head just in time not to miss his answer. He was a rather soft-spoken golem, and I'm pretty sure that I'd somehow misunderstood him. "In the chair?"

*Should I call the county coroner? I mean, I'm sure he's a bit busy, but I really don't think you want melted gray wax to seep into the furniture or the cream rug.*

"Yes, Ms. Raven," Ted exclaimed with a small smile that stretched his thin lips.

"You feel effects of the heat, don't you?" I asked in wonderment, shutting the lid to my laptop. Supernatural details like this never ceased to amaze me. "Is there anything I can do?"

*Yeah, you can shift my fan a little to the right.*

"I'll be fine, Ms. Raven."

Ted awkwardly bent at the waist until his large frame sank into the overstuffed chair. He somehow still managed to keep his back ramrod straight, resting his arms on the armrests to resemble some kind of Lincoln-esque statue.

Before I could ask Ted any more questions about how the heat was affecting his body, a whoosh of air being forced through the vents could be heard in a resounding rush. Leo did a blip, where he was right in front of us one second and gone the next.

I had no doubt that Leo's body was now splayed over top one of the central air vents.

*I'd say this could possibly be better than catnip, but we'd both know that I'd be lying. Can you reach my pipe from where you're sitting?*

"Ted, it's going to take time for the cottage to cool off," I said, setting the laptop back down on the couch while I got up to close most of the windows. I'd leave a couple open to continue to get the cross breeze until the house wasn't quite so stuffy. "Would it help you to remove your jacket?"

I didn't hear Ted's reply over the ringing of my cell phone. It was Heidi. Shooting him an apologetic smile, I answered the call after positioning the phone in between my ear and shoulder.

"We just got air," I exclaimed in delight, figuring Heidi would still stay the night with Jack.

"Listen to me very carefully," Heidi whispered, causing me to stop lowering the side window halfway down. I slowly sank my shoulder back into place once my fingers were once again clutching the phone. What in the world had happened to have Heidi so concerned that she was making a secret call to me? "I need to know the name of the woman who came to visit you a few months ago. You know the one…with the missing familiar?"

"Mazie Rose Young," I whispered back, not knowing why I was mimicking Heidi when I didn't have to worry about being overheard by anyone.

*I'm going to enjoy this cool air coming out of the vent and pretend I didn't hear you say that name.*

I couldn't believe I'd said Mazie's name either, because she wasn't technically a person anymore. I mean, she was…but she'd come to me in the form of a ghost after finding out that Leo and I had solved a few mysteries. I only ever knew her as a spirit.

*Don't even think about her, Raven. The last thing we need is for Mazie to cross through the veil and pay us another visit. I still have that stain on my fur where Strifle left her glittery lip prints.*

Apparently, word had gotten around in the afterlife that Leo and I were successful amateur sleuths of the supernatural. Mazie's familiar—which happened to be a fairy—hadn't crossed through the veil with her as expected. Long story short, a witch who'd wanted Strifle's power had used dark magic to prevent the fairy from crossing over with her host.

Common myth would have some believe that familiars were demons in animal form who served witches. The truth couldn't be further from the story people had been told for centuries. Familiars were kindred spirits who bond with their hosts and share each other's lifetime and health. Familiars could take on a number of physical forms.

*Look, that case is closed. Sealed shut, never to be reopened again. We found Strifle, set her free, and now I'm sullied with glitter on my paw for the rest of my life. Let's leave well enough alone.*

"No, not Mazie," Heidi muttered, her words muffled against the phone. "The older witch who was with her."

*I'm going to pretend I didn't hear that, either. I can't believe I'm saying this about my beloved Heidi…but hang up on her.*

"You mean Lucille?" I asked, walking back over to the couch. Ted hadn't said a word this entire time, but instead he was just observing me very closely with a rather stern frown on his chiseled features. "What about her?"

"I knew I'd recognized the name!" Heidi whispered excitedly, though I wasn't experiencing the same euphoria. "Lucille Rebecca Barnes, right?"

*You couldn't have just hung up the phone, could you? We finally have electricity, and I wasn't even given ten seconds to enjoy the cool inviting air. Not fair, Raven. Not fair at all.*

"This is about the broomstick, isn't it?" I asked hesitantly, using a bit of Leo's cautious tone. "Heidi, what's going on with the investigation?"

*That oaf of a detective is digging into the curse, that's what. I think I would have rather died from heatstroke than be turned into a toad by the council once they find out that we were the ones who led the police right to their front doorstep.*

"Jack thinks the sheriff might have been poisoned with a rare blend of herbs, but he's waiting on the autopsy to confirm his suspicions. That broomstick that was in the man's possession spiked Jack's interest, though. He is looking into some hex, and he reached out to—" Heidi broke off for a brief second. "I've got to go. Raven, call your mother."

Heidi disconnected the line, leaving me hanging without any

information on how to move forward with figuring out if witchcraft was involved with the sheriff's death.

*Oh, my dearest Heidi left you with something...the old "call your mother" trick? Does Heidi not realize that doing the same thing over and over again hoping for a different result is the definition of insanity?*

Technically, the various phone calls I've made to Mom since moving to Paramour Bay had not been so beneficial. Well, in principle, at least.

*If you believe that then I'm relatively sure you are suffering from heatstroke...with permanent lasting effects. Come over to the vent side with me and you'll feel the forced air, Raven. You'll come to your senses once you cool down.*

"Ted, what do you know about curses?" I asked, walking back to the couch to retrieve my laptop. My favorite spot in the living room was sitting on an overstuffed burgundy pillow that I'd positioned in between the coffee table and the fireplace. It was the perfect place to cast magic, but this time I was hoping for a little luck in the research department. "Specifically, a curse on a centuries old broomstick that just might have belonged to Lucille Rebecca Barnes."

*You just had to go and say her name again. I cannot deal with either of those two spirits until I return to a normal temperature, Raven. This has been a very trying day.*

"Dreadful one, that curse," Ted said with a frown.

The only telling sign that the heat had affected him was the tuft of yellowish-blond hair on top of his square head that was out place. Oh, and the fact that he was actually sitting in a chair rather than his normal predilection to hover.

*There are other vents in the house, you know. This cold air is doing wonders for my fur. I would like to apologize for my earlier behavior, though. I might have been a touch out of sorts.*

I was too shocked that Ted might actually know something about the broomstick to respond to Leo's apologetic blurting.

"Ted, are you telling me you know about a cursed broomstick?" I asked, not even bothering to lift the lid on my laptop. I might be able to get all the information I needed from Ted. He never ceased to amaze me. "Did witchcraft actually kill that man?"

"Highly doubtful, Ms. Raven," Ted replied, his frown still in place.

*This cool air has me being somewhat optimistic, Raven. You thought the blackout might have been in connection with magic. We proved otherwise. There are exceptions, of course, but cursed objects are usually just ancient myths with no basis.*

Okay, so both of my so-called advisors were telling me that I might have gone from point A to point Z without considering all the other intersecting points. I breathed a little easier, because preventing Liam and Jack from discovering the supernatural realm might have been almost impossible had the cursed broomstick actually been responsible for the sheriff's death.

"Your mother took care of it," Ted replied.

"Mom took care of what?" I asked guardedly while being pretty sure I was experiencing emotional whiplash of some sort. "Ted, you just said it was doubtful that some curse on a broomstick caused someone's death."

"Yes," Ted agreed, frustrating me even more.

*Uh-oh.*

"Don't you dare *uh-oh* me, Leo," I warned, clearly seeing where this conversation was headed—straight down memory-impaired lane. "Ted, does Mom know about this broomstick?"

"Of course," Ted responded in a tone that signified I already should have known that from his nondescript answers. "Your mother was the one who buried it."

*Yep. I remember now. And if that is the broomstick in question, we're in big trouble right here in River City. B. I. G. with a capital T…and that stands for trouble!*

# Chapter Five

*H*AVE I MENTIONED *lately that I love the benefits of living in the twenty-first century?*

"Leo, have you been laying on that vent all night? You're going to get sick."

I'd set the coffee maker to brew a pot for six-thirty this morning, but it wasn't the delicious aroma that had woken me up this bright and early. As a matter of fact, I don't believe I slept more than a few hours last night at all—especially after Leo's declaration. He'd also been absolutely right, confirmed with one phone call to my mother that had lasted all but three minutes.

*Yes, I've been here all night. And I don't regret a second of this euphoria, although I do believe I'm having some form of catnip withdrawal. Either that, or you were casting spells last night. Also, I can't feel my tail again and am in dire need of the litter box.*

"Maybe that's because you've been lying on your tail for over twelve hours," I said wryly, grabbing a coffee mug out of the cupboard. I debated just drinking it black due to the caffeine intake I was going to need to get through the day, but taking the time to add a bit of sugar wouldn't hurt, either. "Mom should be here in a few minutes."

*Oh, joy. I live to share time with your mother.*

Leo wasn't my mother's biggest fan, and I couldn't blame

him in the least.

*Have you seen my pipe? I'm going to need to smoke a hit of my imported premium organic catnip to get through this domestic ordeal. One could always hope the curse gets me first.*

I completely related to Leo's reaction to my mother's visit, because I was basically fortifying myself with copious amounts of coffee to prepare for the inevitable confrontation.

*Remind me again why we called her in the first place?*

You should understand that it was my mother who'd kept me in the dark about witchcraft. Her feeble effort to protect me had backfired. When she'd left Paramour Bay behind, she'd been pregnant with me. She'd sworn that she was done with a life involving witchcraft, and she raised me to believe there was nothing extraordinary or supernatural about our world. It was all just a fantasy, make believe stories for the movies.

It wasn't until after Nan had passed on and left everything she had—including Leo—to me that I discovered our true lineage. You might say I still harbored a bit of resentment, but the past ten months had taught me a great deal about forgiveness and personal responsibility.

*Raven. I don't believe they're buying all that malarkey. Your mother is actually certifiably insane. It's okay to admit it. There's no shame in admitting the truth. We all have one of those unfortunate odd sorts in the family, and your mother just happened to draw the short straw.*

"I truly believe that Mom thought she was doing what was best for me," I defended, being one of those people who reserved the right to be the only one who could disparage my mother. There was a chance I should take a measure of responsibility for the alleged insanity. I might very well have driven her to it. I do believe that a therapist would have a field day with our family dynamics. Of course, I couldn't discuss any of this with a regular human being. "Being in this world should come with a warning label."

*I wouldn't know about all that…*

I choked on my coffee in a bid to not laugh when Leo finally sat up from laying on the cool vent all night. Needless to say, he looked a bit worse for wear. Certain tufts of hair were standing on end, and I'm pretty sure he had a piece of lint stuck to the end of his nose.

"I totally get it," I replied, leaning back against the counter, changing my mind about drinking my coffee black. A straight shot of caffeine was definitely what I needed today. The Italians were right on the money there. They drank their coffee concentrated, like gunpowder. I was in total agreement that it was the proper way to drink coffee. "If there was any other way to deal with this current mystery, I would. All that changed the second you and Ted finally got around to telling me that Mom had been the one who'd figured out the broomstick in question was cursed…and that she buried it in an attempt to hide it forever."

*Not very well, apparently. If you want the job done right…*

"We need the whole story, and what better way than to go directly to the source?"

With the blackout coming to an end, Liam had been quite busy with helping those older residents reset their breaker boxes and restarting their AC units. He'd texted me a little before midnight, saying that he was just pulling into his driveway with a promise to call me early this morning.

In the meantime, Jack was most likely bringing home Heidi. The state detective would no doubt be following up on the circumstances of the sheriff's death, although I had no idea how long it took to get results from an autopsy. If I were to go by the police shows on television, he'd have already known how the man died in the middle of the town's cobblestone square with the results of numerous complicated lab tests securely in hand.

*Witchcraft.*

"What about witchcraft?"

I was confused as to what Leo was referring to, especially considering he'd just used the litterbox that was positioned next to the washer and dryer in the small nook off the other side of the kitchen. I was almost afraid to hear what my family's abilities had to do with his bodily functions.

*It's a wonder you actually function with that brain pan of yours. Have another cup of coffee, not that I think it'll do you any good. I was answering your initial question about a better way than to drag your mother into this current predicament of yours.*

"Ours," I corrected him with a sideways glance, refusing to be left alone in this endeavor. "You signed on for the whole show, Leo."

*Yours. I was perfectly happy to leave well enough alone in my heatstroke daze, but you just had to ask about the broomstick. Anyway, I was willing to sacrifice my tail for the greater good, but I'm going to have to draw the line somewhere. Cast a spell, find out what we need to know, and then we'll have no use for your mother. C'est la vie.*

There was a small thud against the front door.

I scrunched my nose upon realizing that my mother had a tendency not to knock, but rather just let herself into the cottage. After all, she'd spent most of her childhood living right here in this very home.

Leo sounded as if he were hacking up a hairball, but it was just his belly laugh at the fact that my mother had most likely flattened her face against the brass knocker in her attempt to enter through a locked door.

"Not nice," I muttered, shuffling my slippers across the hardwood floor. "Aren't you the one always talking about karma?"

*Yes, and that was karma at her finest.*

"Morning, Mom," I greeted, barely shifting to the side as my mother breezed right by me and straight into the kitchen. "Good to see you, too."

Physically, it was like looking in a mirror twenty-three years into the future.

The Marigold women not only had the gift of witchcraft, but we all had the same long straight hair that was so black it shimmered blue like a raven's wing. I accepted the green eyes and high cheekbones with grace, but I could have done without the wide hips. Some would say we had hourglass figures, but I argued with that description every time I tried on a pair of tight jeans. Honestly, my hips were the main reason I wore long, flowy skirts.

"You have the wrong broomstick," Mom declared as she set her purse down with a thud on the counter. She didn't even bother to draw air before turning around to open the cupboard and grab a coffee cup. "Whoever told you that the item you saw belonged to Lucille Rebecca Barnes is completely wrong."

*Raven, let me know when you revert to witchcraft instead of listening to half the facts from your mother.*

"Good morning to you as well, Leo." My mother poured some coffee, hedging its taste with a bit of cream and sugar before finally seating herself at the counter without a strand moving in the black head of hair of hers. She always wore it up in a clip, whereas I preferred to wear mine down. "I see you survived the blackout."

*We were fortunate in the culling.*

"Would the two of you stop?" I demanded, seriously in the need of some acetaminophen. A headache was forming that had nothing to do with my dehydration from yesterday's events. "Mom, we have a serious problem on our hands. If Jack or Liam connect the broomstick to the sheriff's death, then all bets are off."

"It's been my experience that mere humans will always have a rational explanation for anything supernatural." My mother calmly sipped her coffee as if we weren't about to be exposed. She gestured that I should join her, but I was too wired to sit. Instead, I walked around the island and leaned my forearms against the granite countertop. "I suggest you leave well enough alone."

*I hate when I'm forced to agree with your mother. It leaves a bitter taste in my mouth.*

"You didn't let me get the entire story out on the phone last night." I set my mug down on the counter and rubbed the sleep from my eyes. "Jack knows that the broomstick belonged to Lucille."

*Regina, don't let her nudge you from your position. I have an entire day of lounging on a cool vent scheduled with my new edibles that should arrive by UPS momentarily. Let the man in the brown shorts sweat. It's his job. I'm sure you have better things to do than chase around ancient myths from your childhood.*

I had been watching my mother's expression very closely, and I could sense this tale of curses wasn't a mere myth. Not that I ever believed that excuse, especially after finding out that my mother had gone to the trouble of burying the item in question.

On a side note, you're probably wondering about my mother's name. All the females in our family have a first name that begins with the letter R. It could be quite confusing at times, but it wasn't like we had family reunions when the majority of us didn't even speak to one another.

*With good reason. Family reunions aren't all they're cracked up to be.*

"Mom," I began to reason once more, completely ignoring Leo's attempt to delay the inevitable. "Trust me when I say that the entire town already knows about the curse. Eileen no doubt told Elsie, who in turn shared the gossip with Wilma. Once those two have a bit of chinwag…all bets are off. I'm just asking for the truth here. Can you tell me why you buried the broomstick without all the usual rigmarole? Not that the runaround isn't fun and all, but I'm a little exhausted from the past twenty-four hours."

*You're using the guilt method. I don't know whether to be offended on Regina's behalf or just proud to be your mentor.*

"Fine," my mother relented, though it was clear she didn't like to conjure up memories from her childhood. "As you know, your grandmother included witchcraft into my everyday studies. I remember there was this lesson regarding cursed objects, and the example she'd chosen was a porcelain doll from the coven in Salem. Quite interesting, really."

*I have a vague memory of that lesson. Your mother was fourteen years old and went around the cottage for weeks thinking every object in sight was cursed…even me, at one point.*

"A fourteen-year-old shouldn't have to run around scared witless," my mother exclaimed cynically before taking another sip of her coffee. Amazingly, her red lipstick didn't leave even a smudge on the rim. "You should be grateful that I spared you the childhood of a young witch."

I wasn't about to get into our usual argument. The only one

who would win in that situation was Leo, and even he'd agreed last night that Jack and Liam shouldn't discover the truth about curses. One thing usually led to another, and Liam was a highly intelligent man. It would only be a matter of time before he connected the dots.

"How did you go from a doll to a broomstick?" I asked, making a mental note to discuss Aunt Rowena after this conversation. She still posed a problem in the grand scheme of things. "And how did Ted know that you buried it? He wasn't even around during your childhood."

My mother arched a perfectly shaped brow and glanced accusingly toward Leo, who'd plopped himself back down over the vent near the spiral staircase. Only his left eye was open, staring back.

*What? I was lonely. I had to talk to someone. In my defense, I don't even remember the conversation. In a better defense, the events of that time with the broomstick are very hazy.*

"Are you saying that you were bored back then?" I inquired with a smile. "Admit it. Your life is much more exciting now that you have me to advise."

*Thrilling. I never know when I'm going to run through my tenth life.*

I couldn't prevent my laugh from bubbling over. I'm pretty sure Leo had used up his nine lives ages ago. His being here at all was thanks to a necromancy spell, and I couldn't be more grateful to Nan for making it happen. He might be a pain in my buttocks at times, but he certainly kept my life exhilarating, too.

"One of my assignments was to research a cursed object, so I decided to go searching for one within our own coven," my mother explained, tilting her head in a manner that told me she'd chosen the Windsor coven on purpose. She'd known how

Nan would have felt about her decision to reach out to the very council who'd excommunicated her. "I was fourteen, Raven. Every teenager pushes back against their mother's limits, and I was no exception."

*See these crooked whiskers? I'm pretty sure the necromancy spell had nothing to do with the kinks in them.*

"Who did you talk to? Aunt Rowena?" I asked with caution, figuring Nan must have been devastated when she'd discovered that my mom had spoken to her former fellow coven members without her permission. "Wait a second. You were fourteen years old. Windsor is over an hour away. How did you even get there?"

"I had friends who were old enough to drive," my mother advised, careful of revealing too much. I'd have to bend Leo's ear later, but I didn't want to delay getting the information I needed to proceed with this case. "I hitched a ride, talked to whoever seemed chatty, and discovered that a particular broomstick was said to be cursed. No one knew what had happened to it, where it was, or who might have had possession of it."

"Wait just a second," I practically gasped, straightening up from the counter. If Leo and Ted knew that my mother had been the one to eventually bury the broomstick, then that could only mean one thing. "You found yourself a mystery to solve. You actually investigated a case of a cursed broomstick, and you loved it!"

*Totally busted!*

"I wouldn't go so far as to say that, my dear." Mom cleared her throat and picked an imaginary piece of lint off of her pristine white blouse. "I was fourteen, living in a small town with a secret. Going out for ice cream was exciting in those days."

*Hmmmm.*

I wanted to ask what Leo was humming about, but I also didn't want to stop my mother from finishing her story. It was hard enough to get her to talk about witchcraft, let alone any exciting shenanigans from when she was younger.

*It's nothing, really. Just some notes I'm keeping for myself.*

"Spit it out," I muttered, needing a refill on my coffee anyway. "Mother, don't think I'm taking your word for it that I should leave the broomstick thing alone."

*I've long since figured out the difference between you and your mother.*

"Me, too. Where would you like me to start?" I asked with a small chuckle that faded after receiving that infamous brow arch from my mother. I cleared my throat as I made the decision to add cream and sugar to my coffee for this next round. "Leo?"

*Easily detectable, now that I think about it. The secret of your family weighed heavily on Regina's shoulders, and she was serious when undertaking every endeavor. You? Well, you blurted your secret out to Heidi in record time and dove headfirst into this sleuthing business. Your do-good meter is off the charts, whereas your mother's self-preservation ranked higher above all else.*

"Self-preservation was what had me burying that darn broomstick in the first place." My mother slid her mug over the counter for a refill. Seeing as I already had out the cream and sugar, it didn't take me long to make her another cup of coffee. "After a bit of digging—no pun intended, dear—I was able to trace the broomstick back to a descendant of the Barnes family. This older woman had died, though the authorities had assumed it was due to heart failure. There was an estate auction soon afterward, and all of the woman's belongings had been sold off. It took me all summer to figure out who bought the broomstick, but by then it was too late."

"Too late…you mean *dead* too late?"

*Speaking of late, the UPS man should have been here by now. He better not have skipped out with my edibles.*

"Well, yes." Mom paused to take a sip of the coffee I'd made her, her pinky automatically lifting into the air. "The man who'd purchased many items from the estate sale had fallen off a ladder and died at the hospital a few short days later. At that time, I figured it was best to explain to your grandmother what I'd discovered in my research."

*Speaking of research, would you hop online and check the tracking number on my shipment? It cost you a lot of money, you know. It would be a shame not to receive it.*

"What happened then?" I asked, settling my forearms back onto the granite. I felt like that little girl at Christmas when her parents told stories from their childhood. I'd been denied these family tales until the age of thirty, and even then getting my mother to talk was like taking a chisel to a boulder. "What was Nan's reaction?"

"Pride mixed with sheer horror," Mom explained with what I thought might very well be a fond smile. "Well, I'd wanted to utilize a spell to get rid of the curse. Your grandmother was quick to explain that curses were a bit more complex than that, and one shouldn't try to outdo another witch's ritual handiwork. Apparently, there was only one recourse."

*Speaking of recourse, there's going to be an even higher price to pay if that UPS driver doesn't show up in the next five minutes.*

"Seriously?" I straightened up from the counter, refusing to believe that Nan of all witches would have taken the easy way out. "You just buried the broomstick."

"Yes, I did."

*Wait! I hear an engine.*

Leo's short legs scrambled to get a footing underneath him as he waddled from the vent to the bay window facing the front drive. Instead of attempting to jump up to his pillow, which took him quite a few tries, he disappeared in the blink of an eye only to reappear on his favorite cat bed.

*Forget everything I said about that UPS driver. He's a saint in brown shorts. He resisted temptation to run away with the most delicious catnip edibles one can buy, only to deliver it to little ol' me. I'm telling you, the man deserves a raise for all his hard work.*

"Raven, I'm beginning to get concerned that you've allowed Leo's addiction to get out of control," Mom said foolishly, not understanding Leo's relationship with the minty herb. I related, because the coffee bean was the best thing to ever grow out of the earth's rich soil. "Have you—"

*Look, witch traitor. I will have you know that—*

"Okay, then," I said, shooting Leo a warning glance that told him not to spar with my mother before I was able to get more information regarding Lucille's broomstick. "Leo, let me grab your package off the front porch. Mom, where did you bury the broomstick and how were you able to touch it without suffering the consequences?"

"Touching it doesn't kill a person, dear," my mother replied as if she were giving me a history lesson. "Having it in one's possession for a longer period of time is what accomplishes the deed, though I have no idea how many days or months that might take."

*Why don't you go get it and find—*

Leo did his disappearing act when I veered in his direction instead of the door. Satisfied that he wasn't going to finish that sentence, I quickly retrieved his package from the front stoop with a quick wave to the driver. He was already in his truck and ready to continue along his route, leaving me to wonder if he had room in the passenger seat. Honestly, a nice vacation before the end of summer was sounding better and better.

"If you say one more word to instigate her, I will toss your stash of catnip down the garbage disposal," I muttered, my reverie of a sandy beach dissipating upon the sound of a discreet cough. I opened up the package with my car keys that were in the wooden bowl I kept on top of the narrow table next to the front door. "Eat your treat and be quiet."

I left Leo to enjoy his morning snack, snatching up my coffee cup before rejoining my mother at the kitchen island. Her irritation with Leo was obvious from her pursed lips and the deep lines in her forehead.

"Back to the broomstick," I prodded, pulling out the stool next to my mother. "What else can you tell me about it? Clearly, someone dug it up by accident. I have no idea how the sheriff got ahold of it, but Liam and Jack are relatively sure that the sheriff who died had been poisoned."

"Poisoned?" Mom asked in astonishment, setting her mug down on the granite with a click. "Usually, a death in relation to the curse is more of the natural variety, like a heart attack or stroke. Poison is…"

"Murder."

*What is with your affinity of the M word? Seriously, can't a familiar get one minute of peace enjoying the better things in life without his charge throwing herself headfirst into a murder mystery? And your mother wonders why I need copious amounts of my select organic catnip. Well, now you know, Regina. Now you know—it's living with your offspring.*

# Chapter Six

"DID YOU HEAR about that poor sheriff?" Pearl Saffron shook her head in dismay as she looked over the specialty teas I'd received in my inventory earlier this week. "Poison. Such a horrible way to go. Eileen told Beverly, who in turn told Cora that Heidi's detective received confirmation that Sheriff O'Leary died from ingesting some kind of poison."

No one had received confirmation, but I didn't bother to correct Pearl. She shuddered in horror as she lifted her reading glasses that were hanging around her neck by a silver chain. She'd recently switched what jewelry she was wearing to all silver or white gold, afraid that the yellow gold would clash with her hair dye…which just so happened to be purple.

*She's color blind, anyway. Back to this mystery that might not be such a mystery after all—Sheriff O'Leary might have enjoyed a daily dose of saccharin with his morning coffee. It could happen. People are strangely odd that way. That stuff is deadly if used repeatedly. They say it can build up in the brain and cause dementia. There's nothing to prove it was related to simple plants and herbs, so there might not be any mystery to solve, if that's the case.*

There was definitely a mystery to solve, but I was limited in using witchcraft. The curse on the broomstick would most likely prevent me from utilizing the item to conjure up the sheriff's last living moments. It was highly doubtful that I would be able to get access to the personal belongings he'd had on his body at the time of his death.

Due to the limitations that I was currently facing and the fact that I needed to figure out a strategy with at least some likelihood of success, I'd opened the tea shop this morning as usual. These side investigations always had to come in second to my livelihood, which was one of the reasons I'd hired Beetle as my part-time helper. I used those hours he was at the helm to cast cantrip level magic on special tea blends for various customers, and there were times I applied that free time to solve the occasional murder.

*Your time could be put to better use…such as reading over your lessons I've mapped out for the week. Your studies suffer when you become Nancy Drew. An example would be Justine Davis, who keeps getting a rash on the palms of her hands. Being the only seamstress in town, it might behoove you to protect those fingers of hers with an herbal remedy. Clearly the dead sheriff might have devoured bags of saccharine to keep him awake on some stakeout. Like I said, there might not be a mystery to solve.*

I'd resolved a while ago that being a witch and having access to magic shouldn't go to waste. Nan had applied her gift to holistic remedies to aid in her customers' health, and I'd continued with that family tradition. But there was so much more I could do for the greater good—like solving the community's mysteries.

*I'm pretty sure those good intentions should be reserved for those witches who aren't novices or highly accident-prone. Those who are could very well end up as the victim in one of those murder mysteries.*

"Did you know Sheriff O'Leary personally?" I asked, coming around the counter so that I could help Pearl make a choice based on her past purchases. I also wondered if there was some way to get information on the man's family. Having solved a few mysteries over the course of my ten months as a witch, I'd come to find that family and friends were usually the first suspects. As for Leo's mention of me being a bit accident-prone…isn't everyone when they first start out? "Having lost Nan, I completely understand their grief."

*Is now the time to point out that you barely spoke a word to your grandmother for close to twelve years before she died? And since you were the one to bring up the question in regard to blundering your way through your lessons, then no—clumsiness has not been bestowed on everyone equally. You might say that you have a gift.*

In my defense, my accident-prone abilities sometimes were the very reason our cases were solved.

*I need a minute to come up with my own defense. Debating with you is like suffering from vertigo. I defer to my default adage— even a blind squirrel finds a nut every once in a while.*

"I know of the O'Learys, but their little town is close to forty minutes away. It's not all that different from Paramour Bay. They came to this year's Spring Festival, though. Didn't you notice the redhead sitting down two tables from you? Deidre O'Leary co-owns the antique store here in town with her sister, which is probably why the sheriff was visiting Kathleen—the blonde one."

*Purple Pearl would have to bring up the Spring Festival. I still have nightmares about that killer clown, and now you want to go and bring up those horrifying memories so that I suffer from insomnia once again. You people are appalling.*

"Dandelion tea? I haven't tried this one yet," Pearl said with excitement, though I wasn't sure that was the right blend for her to try this week. I reached over and chose a less caffeinated blend, and one that had a similar taste to the pumpkin blend she usually preferred. Her smile faded when she realized that it wasn't her usual pumpkin spice. "Oh, I do miss my favorite flavor. When will you be getting it back into the shop?"

*I'd just like to point out that you're responsible if Purple Pearl keels over from a heart attack. Don't think I don't know why you stocked up on that dandelion tea blend.*

"Late September to early October," I responded distractedly, tapping the pen I'd had in my hand against my chin. I also made no excuse for my love of the dandelion tea leaves. It had the caffeine kick of coffee, but I'd recently read an article that stated a couple cups of coffee a day were good for the heart. "So, Sheriff O'Leary was here to visit his sister-in-law. I'm surprised I didn't see Kathleen outside after Monty found that poor man's body in the middle of town square."

*Do you believe everything you read? The UFO sighting in Roswell was in the paper, too.*

"That's because Kathleen wasn't at the store yesterday morning. She'd gone into Branford for an estate sale, hoping to pick up some pieces for the shop. At least, that's what she claimed. I'm sure she was holed up in some swanky air-conditioned auction hall as she allowed her assistant to mind the shop. Lydia does so much for that woman." Pearl still kept ahold of the dandelion tea leaves, and she also took the one I'd offered in replacement of her favorite blend. She patted the boxes. "I'm all set with these two."

That sliver of excitement I experienced when I was close to piecing together a clue began to flutter in my stomach. Why had Sheriff O'Leary been visiting his sister-in-law? And if she hadn't been in the shop, just what had he and her assistant discussed? Had Lydia sold him the broom, or had he brought it with him?

Had she been the one to give him the list of herbs that could possibly poison a person?

*I'm so going to need to hit the catnip today, aren't I? Hey, where's my BFF? There's a thunderstorm coming in off the bay. It's the perfect type of weather to lounge around and think over how your spontaneous decisions usually have us dipping a toe in our own graves.*

"I think it's wonderful that Deidre and Kathleen are business owners together," I said, hoping to keep Pearl talking about the sisters. "Keep it in the family, right?"

"Don't let those two girls fool you." Pearl had followed me back to the counter, where she set the two boxes next to the cash register. "They're like oil and water. I don't think they've ever agreed on anything. Deidre has a temper unlike any other from what I hear, but Kathleen is more cunning. It's the reason she runs the shop and her sister stays out of the day-to-day decisions. We like it that way, of course, hence why no one really knows the O'Learys on a personal level. Kathleen's surname is Reynolds."

*Before you go blaming my short-term memory loss for not remembering any of these details, the blonde lady took over the antique shop right before my beloved Rosemary crossed through the veil. Then you came into my life…which, in case you hadn't noticed, has kept me rather busy. My grasp of the idle gossip in Paramour Bay seems to have suffered as a result.*

Pearl was already counting out the dollar bills needed to pay for her items, while I was trying to sort through the numerous questions flying through my mind.

"Do you know Kathleen well?" I asked, taking my time making change from the money Pearl had given me. "I met her a couple of times at the town hall meetings, but I'd just assumed she was a native. I'll be sure to send a note in condolence."

"I've stopped into the shop from time to time," Pearl replied, though it was clear she'd had ulterior motives for such visits. Paramour Bay was a close-knit community, and they tended to do a bit of investigating before accepting any strangers. "Kathleen seems genuine, and she does a rather good job with keeping her sister at arm's length. That's good enough for me."

That would explain why the residents of town knew of the O'Leary clan, but didn't truly know them like they did Kathleen. Interesting. Very interesting.

*I think it's time you call my BFF on the phone. He should have been here by now, and I believe I'm getting a tic in my sensitive whisker.*

"Here you are." I had already handed Pearl back her change and slipped her purchases into the brown paper bag I'd had my shop's name branded on in the same calligraphy that was hand-painted on the shop's window. "Please remember to go easy on the dandelion blend. It has more caffeine than what you're used to with your other favorite tea leaves."

"Oh, really?" Pearl exclaimed with a wink.

*What was that for? Please tell Purple Pearl to stop that right this instant. She reminds me of that song...the* Purple People Eater. *What has she done? Now I'm going to have that song stuck in my head all day.*

"Maybe I'll finally be able to keep up with Harold," Pearl said with a light laugh, leaving me to try and block out the image of her with her new beau in the throes of passion. "Ta-ta!"

*I blame you entirely. This just keeps getting worse.*

"I've just made Harold a very happy man," I amended with a smile.

*There's something wrong with you. Why do you need to paint these pictures in my head? It's just flat out cruel.*

"And you wouldn't have it any other way," I replied, glancing outside the display window. It was only going on ten-thirty in the morning, but one would never know it from the way the clouds had blocked the sun. Leo was right about that thunderstorm. I wasn't going to want to go outside anytime soon. I couldn't leave the store anyway, but that didn't mean that Leo was stuck here. "I need you to do me a favor."

*And I need my catnip, but you don't see me getting what I want today, either. I also don't see my BFF here with my morning edible. It looks as if we're both fresh out of luck.*

"Technically, you're the only one out of luck," I corrected, leaning on the counter so that I could see him better. "Your short-term memory is on the fritz again. Don't you remember that Mom took Beetle to breakfast this morning? They're also spending the rest of the day together, and I do not—under any circumstances—want to know what they're doing with their time."

*You're making that connection again, right?*

Leo had been linking his good memory days with those mornings he ingested his premium organic catnip. Unfortunately, he was forgetting that he'd already consumed a small portion before we'd even left the cottage.

*It's not the same stuff, and you know it. There's a very specific difference.*

"The catnip that Beetle buys for you is no different than the stuff you get from Honduras." We'd been over this a million times, but Leo refused to believe that Beetle wasn't some divinity when it came to catnip. "In the meantime, I need you to do your invisible act and go see what's happening in the antique shop."

*First, when did my thing become an* act? *Secondly, why would I do that?*

I was startled by the streak of lightning that shot across the sky. It wasn't uncommon to get storms after such a heatwave, and I was very grateful that we'd had our power restored yesterday. Hopefully, we made it through the incoming storm without being thrown back into darkness. The palm of my hand began to tingle, but I ignored it in my bid to talk Leo into going to the antique shop.

"I need to know if Kathleen is in the shop today." I highly doubted that Kathleen would be working, given that her brother-in-law just died yesterday. With that said, it didn't sound as if the two sisters had been getting along lately. Maybe there was a chance I could stop in and find out a little more about the broomstick and where the sheriff had found such a cursed object. "It will only take you a few minutes to—"

The fading sound of the air conditioner slowly dying had both Leo and I looking at one another in horror.

*Tell me that wasn't what I think it was, Raven. I can't handle another day of being in a sauna. You and I both know I've already used up my nine lives.*

The overhead lights blinked once…then twice and done.

Finished.

Kaput.

We'd definitely lost power.

That horrible sensation of a heavy rock settling in my stomach hit me with a thud.

*Your request is going to have wait, Raven. Before I lose my all my energy to the extreme forces of Mother Nature's heat, I'm going after Skippy and his band of ninja squirrels. They are not going to get away with this a second time!*

Leo's backend was already wiggling back and forth as if he

were getting ready to pounce.

"Leo, I don't think—"

And just like that, Leo disappeared to continue his eternal war with the resident squirrels. What he didn't know was that right before we lost power, I'd had a sliver of static electricity pierce the palm of my hand.

Skippy and his band of merry miscreants weren't responsible for the second blackout.

The minute my cell phone began to ring, I knew who was solely accountable for such a calamity—my mother.

# Chapter Seven

"YOU DON'T EVEN like using...you know what," I practically hissed into the phone. Karen Finley had entered the tea shop the second I'd answered my phone. She was pretending to browse while I talked in a hushed tone. "Mother, fix this mess right now!"

I couldn't believe that my mother had harnessed energy for some type of spell during a thunderstorm. Leo hadn't been too concerned in the beginning of my lessons, given my level of experience, to explain to me that casting magic during thunderstorms was dangerous. It was easy to draw too much energy too quick.

Now?

I was getting stronger and more confident with each passing day.

Leo had gone on and on about the dangers associated with utilizing magic during unpredictable weather just last week, especially after witnessing the petals circling above the pestle during my creation of an herbal remedy. I'd been so concentrated on the spell that I hadn't realized I'd created a mini-tornado of white rose petals inside my living room.

If I was able to do that with just a few gathering clouds, then no wonder my mother had been able to short circuit an entire town with the severe weather we were having.

"Please tell me that Beetle isn't with you." I closed my eyes and held my breath for her answer, feeling more like Leo every second that passed—stressed, frazzled, and waiting for the other shoe to drop from high up above.

"We're actually at your cottage right this minute, and I stepped outside to speak with Ted about gathering some material components for a spell you'd be able to use on the dirt from where I'd buried the broom," my mother explained before discreetly coughing.

That telltale sign told me that she'd done something I wasn't going to like...such as descending the town into darkness.

"Are you finding everything just fine, Mrs. Finley?" I asked, holding the cell phone down on my shoulder while I checked in with my customer. She flashed me a smile and waved that I should continue with my personal phone call. It wasn't very professional of me, but I was definitely in a bind. I scrambled to put the phone back to my ear. "Mom, why did the power go out if you were waiting for me to help with the incantation? Plus, we didn't even obtain dirt from the burial site yet...right?"

"Well, dear, I might have made a slight detour before arriving in town this morning."

My mother's next words were muffled, which ratcheted up my stress level nearly to the breaking point.

"Mother, explain yourself this instant," I whispered harshly, wishing I were at the cottage with her and Beetle. The thought of Beetle finding out that we were witches had me breaking out into hives. It was one thing for Heidi to know, but Beetle was utterly unpredictable. "You stopped at the place where you buried the...item? Are you kidding me right now? You didn't think to mention this to me before I opened for business?"

"Thank you, Ted," my mother replied to the individual

she'd been conversing with while I almost went blue from holding my breath. Those two didn't even like one another. "I didn't tell you about my little detour because of this very reason—you tend to overreact over such trivial things. It's you, dear, who would have jumped headfirst into a divination spell without considering the ramifications. You need to find your own rhythm…your natural tempo."

I pulled my cell phone away from my ear and could only stare at the device in disbelief. Overreact? Rhythm? Tempo? My mother—the very witch who professed to give up her craft—just caused a massive blackout during an epic thunderstorm. How in the world was it in her head that I was the spontaneous one?

The rest of the call was so going to have to be made in private. I quietly slipped through the string of beads that blocked the back room off from sight and hearing. The enchanted ivory-colored fairy beads would prevent anyone in the main shop from hearing a single word I said…and there were going to be a few choice sentences I was about to string together for my mother to understand the level of wrath my simmering anger had reached. It was currently at a boiling point.

"You just took out the town's power, Mother." I rested my hand on top of my head in exasperation, wondering how such a wonderful week had spiraled out of control. "Fix it. Now."

*I have searched high and low for that hairy rat, but Skippy and his band of ninja squirrels are nowhere to be found. I don't get it. You'd think they'd be celebrating for getting one over on me.*

Leo plopped himself on the high-top counter in the inventory room, a bit overheated from his recent search. He splayed himself out so that his chin was level with the hard surface. His bulging left eye eventually focused on me, awaiting my response.

*Why do you look like that? Wait. Don't answer that. I didn't ask, and I don't want to know. Strike that. I shouldn't know. As a matter of fact, I was thinking of reserving a one-way airplane ticket to Honduras to inspect this year's crop of catnip. From the pallor of your skin, I'd say there's a slim chance I might actually be able to talk you into packing a bag and coming with me.*

"In my defense, I was inside Ted's shack in the backyard when I began to cast the spell," my mother said, without an ounce of real apology in her tone. I could even picture the way she tilted her chin when being confronted with an accusation. "I had no idea a storm was rolling in over the bay or else I never would have attempted such an intricate incantation that needs such a delicate balance. By the way, I'll be happy to pay for the repair of damage to the side of the house and have some of those vines replanted."

The way Leo's whiskers began to twitch, I started to wonder if he was finally going to lose his grip on his sanity. It wasn't like I could blame him. Interacting with my mother was like asking to be put onto one of those swirling teacups at Disney-land…only at a high rate of speed.

"I'd ask how you missed the fact that grey clouds have been moving in for the last hour or that lightning streaks have been shooting across the sky, but I'm afraid you'll actually answer me." I definitely didn't want to know the extent of damage to my beautiful vines. I quickly formed a plan, because these residents didn't deserve to suffer from the heat all because my mother had forgotten one of the cardinal rules of witchcraft. "It's not like we can utilize a spell right now with the thunderstorm practically on top of us, so we'll wait until it passes before you fix this. In the meantime, please tell me that Beetle has no clue about…"

I was waving my hand in the air, because I couldn't figure

out what exactly I wanted reassurance about first—that my part-time employee hadn't discovered that the Marigold women were witches, had finally noticed that Ted was actually a wax golem, or that there was still a hexed broom out there waiting to claim its next victim.

There was also the fact that Leo had still yet to say a word, which really worried me. As a matter of fact, his whiskers had completely stopped twitching. He was simply staring off into space, as if he'd gone to some faraway place in his mind that didn't involve magic, flubbed-up spells, nor power outages.

"Beetle was inside the cottage the entire time, even after the lightning had struck," my mother reassured me, taking great pains to keep optimism in her tone. I recognized it right away as she continued to try and set my mind at ease that things weren't all that bad. "The minute the storm passes, I'll restore the power grid immediately. In the meantime, you'll be happy to know that I saw who unearthed the broomstick."

That was the first piece of good news I'd all day. I leaned forward and poked my head through the ivory-colored fairy beads after I'd heard the bell above the door. Sure enough, the tea shop had another customer. It seemed we were getting a rush.

"Mom, I've got several customers." I waved toward Karen and her husband, receiving the gesture in kind. "Tell me who found the location of the broomstick and dug it up out of the ground, and then I'll try to slip that information to Liam. Maybe someone knew of the curse and wanted Sheriff O'Leary dead."

"I find it hard to believe that Sheriff O'Leary's own deputy wanted him dead."

I yanked my head back through the ivory-colored fairy beads, causing them to dance together in a melodic rhythm.

"Did the deputy stumble across the broomstick sticking out

of the ground or something? We've been getting storms, so it's possible that the ground had been disturbed." I was hoping that was the case, but my mother's silence told me otherwise. "You're about to tell me that the deputy seemed to be looking specifically for the broomstick, aren't you?"

I glanced at Leo, but he was still looking a bit worse for wear.

"We both know that what we see while casting a divination can easily be misconstrued," my mother warned, still having no compunction over the fact the town had once again been descended into the Dark Ages over her inattentiveness to the weather. "I've done my part to help you with this mystery, my dear. Having been the one to bury the hexed object, I only felt it right to determine who unearthed it."

*I have a lot of feelings about your mother right now. Shall I lament those spirits?*

It was really good to have Leo back, because he really needed to make his way down to the antique store for a quick look around. The sooner I was able to talk with Kathleen, the faster I would be able to figure out how Sheriff O'Leary's deputy knew about the cursed broomstick and where to find it.

"You're not going anywhere until the storm passes and you fix this power failure," I warned my mother, taking time to reach over Leo to the small cubbies where I kept the enchanted blends. Otis came in once a week for his holistic mixture to help with his arthritis. "So stay right there, and I'll be home after I close up the shop."

I disconnected the line before my mother could say another word and throw a wrench into the game plan. Liam had called earlier to tell me he'd stop by the tea shop on his way to meet Jack, but I wasn't so sure that would be the case now the town had once again lost power. I'd have to call him after ringing up

Karen and Otis' order. I didn't want to be a step ahead of the police and let something slip that I couldn't explain.

A deep inhalation and a ten-second meditation had me ready to pass back through the ivory-colored fairy beads.

*Not so fast there, little Miss Nancy Drew.*

"I was thinking more Daphne, because right now you've got to be Scooby-Doo. So, shoo on over to the antique store and see if Kathleen is there, and I'll figure out some excuse to go and talk to her." I reached around and drew my long black hair over my left shoulder, smoothing it down so that I appeared to be composed after all but disappearing on the Finleys. It wouldn't do to have them believing I was a bit woo-woo. "Maybe Sheriff O'Leary told her why his deputy was out in the middle of nowhere digging up a hexed object."

*Woo-woo? What is this?* Practical Magic?

"Hey, I loved that movie," I whispered, quickly leaving Leo before he could say another word. He'd recovered from learning that my mother had used magic at the exact moment a major thunderstorm rolled through the area, and the fact that she'd done so while Beetle had been within shouting distance. "Sorry about that, Mr. and Mrs. Finley. I was just collecting your order. How is your arthritis holding up, Mr. Finley?"

*Better than mine. I've got one massive pain right in the middle of my—*

"Better than ever." Otis beamed, patting his fishing vest. He had no idea that he'd cut off one of Leo's infamous, if not long-winded, lectures. "This storm was supposed to pass us by, but it seemed to turn at the last minute. Can't believe we lost power again."

*Oh, I can believe it. You know why? Because your mother—*

"I have cash," Karen said, holding up her wallet. I continued to smile, though my lips were beginning to feel like I'd had Botox injected in them just a few minutes ago. It didn't help that Leo came strolling out through the beads, his ungraceful exit catching the Finleys' attention. "There's that handsome tomcat of yours. I'm glad to see that he's not outside with the incoming storm, Raven."

*I'll tolerate Mrs. Finley, only because she recognizes my rogue good looks. As for your assumption that I was going to give you a lecture on your mother...you'd have been correct, but not for the reasons you think. You see, dear Raven, your mother was the complete opposite of you. She was one of the most cautious young witches of her time, always triple checking every single component to a spell before she ever uttered the first word.*

"We best be heading out before we can't see a foot in front of us," Otis said, reaching for the bag I'd placed their items in after taking the cash Karen had retrieved from her wallet. "Let's hope the power isn't out as long as it was yesterday."

"Be safe," I called out, waiting until the glass door was closed all the way and the Finleys were out of sight before addressing the horrible assumption that Leo had just made regarding my mother. "Leo, you cannot think for one minute that—"

*There is no rationalizing this, Raven. Your mother is much too skilled to cast a spell during unpredictable weather. Now, she wants us to believe that she gave up witchcraft after leaving home all those years ago, but we both know that's not true. She was just very good at hiding the Marigold way of life around you. Now that you've come to the dark side, she clearly feels she can allow her druthers to hang out everywhere.*

Druthers?

Wow, I hadn't heard that word used in a very long time, but I also had never looked at my mother from Leo's perspective.

Was he right?

Had my mother utilized her magic for her own gain, not caring that she could have done a lot worse than descend the town into darkness? Was she losing her inhibitions?

*Of course, I'm right. I'm always right. Why do you continue to question me on these types of things?*

My brow subconsciously raised in the same way Mom's eyebrow did when trying to prove a point. It was automatic. Most of my mannerisms came from my mother, and my heart began to pound frantically against my chest with the thought that...

*There are a lot of reasons my anxiety is at an asthma-inducing level, but the thought of you turning into Regina isn't one of them. Now, only one of us can lose our grip on our sanity at a time. That's me. I reserved that particular spot a long time ago. Our most pressing issue right now is the fact that your mother was covering up her own tracks by attempting to figure out who dug up that broomstick. Meanwhile, lightning struck the cottage where I store my premium organic catnip. This poses a national threat, Raven.*

"Which could only mean Mom did something really bad back then," I whispered in horror, nausea forcing me to sit on the stool. "Leo, what are we going to do?"

*I never thought I'd say this...I have a bugout bag.*

"What? Mom's negligence might have gotten someone killed, Leo. We can't just leave." My thoughts were now spinning in a million different directions. I flattened the palms of my hands on the counter for some semblance of balance. If what we were considering held even an ounce of truth, wouldn't my right palm be burning with the energy of the earth? Or was it simply that I couldn't accept that Mom might have done something horrible way back when? "How do we solve a case where Mom is one step ahead of us?"

*Rowena.*

I could only stare at Leo with incredulity as he barely managed to mumble the name of who was basically our nemesis. Aunt Rowena wanted to split the coven in two and lead one of the factions to dominate the other. It was her own twisted way of making restitution to Nan, but Aunt Rowena's methods meant putting a lot of lives at risk. We wanted nothing to do with her, and our current problem shouldn't change our opinions.

"Who are you, and what have you done with my undead familiar?"

*Funny, Raven. Real funny, but we are now at a point where we need to one-up the Queen Marigold. We need to fight lightning with lightning. In case it escaped you, Rowena's attitude is practically the proverbial rod on the roof. She can singe your mother's plan into embers with just one look, much like our vines.*

"Aunt Rowena has been visiting Mom in the city quite recently in her bid to get Mom to join her faction. What if there is more to the story?"

*It's a chance we'll need to take, because your mother just descended Paramour Bay into darkness. There's no telling what she'll do next, Raven. I'll be back soon.*

Leo disappeared, but I immediately called him back. Additional tufts of fur were sticking up on his head, and he wobbled on the counter.

*Don't do that! It's hotter than Hades out there, so make it quick.*

"That's the point," I said, knowing Leo better than he knew himself. I would be lucky to see him again before nightfall. "You're going to get to Aunt Rowena's house where it's nice and cool, and you're not going to want to leave. I know how this works, Leo."

He tried unsuccessfully to squint his left eye.

"Don't give me that look," I warned him, not wanting to spend the rest of the day believing my mother would actually stoop so low as to cover up some witchcraft snafu she might have been part of back in the day. "State our position, and then come right back here."

I'm pretty sure Leo mumbled that there was no escaping Hades, but he'd vanished before I could make out the rest of his incoherent sentence. The silence of the shop became almost deafening as I continued to try and come up with a reason why Mom would risk herself and anyone in the vicinity of a spell just to find out who dug up the broomstick.

A crack of lightning suddenly lit up the entire street in front of the shop. I put a hand to my chest, as if I could steady my racing heartbeat. What caught my eye through the display window practically had my heart skidding to a complete halt.

Liam was running from his truck to the front door of the police station to avoid the rain that had begun coming down in torrents. That wasn't what had stone-cold fear overtaking my body until I could barely breathe. The terror that flooded my veins was due to the item clutched in his right hand—the hexed broomstick itself.

# Chapter Eight

"…GO ON HOME, Eileen."

"Are you sure? This is when we get the most calls from the residents. They usually just ask questions about how long it will take for the power to return, but you'll be busy helping the elderly townsfolk with one thing or another."

"And it's nothing I can't handle," Liam reassured Eileen from somewhere back in his partially lit office from what I assume was some source of limited power to keep the phone lines working, along with a few emergency lights. "You and I both know it'll be the same townsfolk who call in for the same reasons every time something like this happens. Go and buy your bags of ice before the gas station runs—"

Liam had reappeared on the shadowy threshold of his office door, looking down at a file in his hand when he finally noticed that he and Eileen weren't alone. A bright smile formed on his handsome face, but I found it hard to return his enthusiasm when I somehow had to convey to him that he needed to get rid of the hexed broomstick.

"Raven, you poor dear. Here. Hand me your umbrella," Eileen ordered while ushering me through the swinging counter door that hadn't been taken out during the numerous renovations that must have taken place over the decades. The dispatcher's heavy dose of perfume hit me before I could brace myself. "Can you believe that we lost power again? Goodness gracious, I don't think I've ever seen anything like this before in all my years growing up here."

My hair and clothes were mostly dry, given that I'd used an umbrella to walk from the tea shop to the police station. It was still somewhat cooler inside after coming in from the rain, but it was easy to tell that the humidity was rising with each passing second the main power remained off and the central air wasn't working. There were two lanterns stationed on a nearby desk that used fuel oil. I'm sure they were positioned there as backup in case their small generator ran out of gas. I handed off my umbrella, still trying to figure out what I was going to say to Liam about the broomstick.

"Thanks, Eileen." I locked gazes with Liam and forced another smile, but I'm not so sure I covered my apprehension. Who am I kidding? I was absolutely terrified that he still had the cursed broomstick in his possession. "I just saw Monty closing up his shop, as well as Bree locking up at the bakery. After yesterday, I don't think anyone wants to chance going over eighteen hours without power."

"I don't blame them," Eileen said, grabbing her oversized purse from her desk drawer. She cast Liam a worried glance. "Are you sure that you don't want me to stay?"

"Go," Liam instructed with a fond smile. "I'll see you tomorrow. I'll forward the phones if I have to leave the office."

Eileen didn't waste any more time as she skedaddled right through the swinging counter door, out the front exit, and headed straight to her vehicle. It wasn't until she'd driven off that I finally turned my attention back to Liam. He'd leaned a shoulder against the doorframe, most likely wearing my same expression of concern.

"What's wrong, Raven?"

"Do you trust me?" The anxious words came out of my mouth before I was able to run them through my filter. I could actually answer for him, because he shouldn't trust me. All I'd done from the moment I laid eyes on him was pile one lie on top of another. It was probably best if I reworded the question before he replied. "If I asked you to do something truly important to me, would you do it with no questions asked?"

Liam seemed to weigh my words, as if he understood that the undertone of my question had an additional layer of significance which hadn't been stated.

Without replying, he held out his hand.

I'm not sure if my reaction to his response had been delayed from yesterday's shock at thinking Liam might be dead or if I really just needed the reassurance that he would still accept me should the truth come finally out.

Each step I took became quicker until I was in his embrace, inhaling his woodsy scent as if I'd never again have a chance to do so again.

"Hey, whatever it is...it can't be that bad," Liam murmured against my ear. I could feel the folder in his hands resting on my back, but it didn't take away from the comfort he was providing me. He allowed me to remain in his arms until I was finally ready to give back some of his personal space. I'm pretty sure the temperature had risen another two or three degrees in that short time span. He used his thumb to brush away a strand of hair before meeting my gaze. "You want the truth?"

My heart skidded to a stop, and I wasn't so sure it was going to beat again.

Was Liam saying that he didn't trust me?

What if I couldn't convince him that the broomstick might

be the very reason why Sheriff O'Leary had died in the middle of the town's square?

I found myself nodding my head in response, even though I was scared beyond belief that this would be it—the end.

"I've always known you were keeping something from me, Raven." Liam sighed in what almost sounded like defeat, but he showed no physical signs that he was ready to give in. Instead, he took my hand and drew me deeper into his office. He didn't stop until I was seated in one of the two guest chairs. The other one was filled with files, which meant that Liam was looking for something specific. "I figured all this time that you'll tell me when you're ready. Trust is a two-way street, and I've been an open book with you. I've done everything humanly possible to show you that I'm in this for the long haul, and that I'm trustworthy. I've been falling more in love with you every single day, Raven Lattice Marigold. Telling you that in the middle of another blackout wasn't in my original plans, but you have a way of muddling those kinds of things up for me."

I wasn't sure whether to laugh, cry, dance, or run away as fast as I could all at the same time.

Liam knelt before me, taking my hands in his after he'd dropped the file on his desk. He lifted my fingers and gently pressed his warm lips to my knuckles.

"I do trust you, Raven, but I need you to show yours in return," Liam said, his dark gaze focused solely on me. This was it. The moment that I'd feared and hoped for all at once, and I wasn't ready to make the choice. "Let me put it to you this way—the only one who might walk out that door is you. I'm not going anywhere."

*I believe we've reached another level of Hades. Is it possible for catnip to melt? I bet we're close to finding out. I'll tell you, Raven, I* came very close to staying in the cool kitchen of Rowena's residence. Of course, it only took me two seconds to change my mind. That woman can induce an asthma attack faster than your harebrained witchy antics.

Leo had returned, and all I wanted to do was scream for him to leave. He'd try to change my mind, and I needed to make this monumental decision on my own.

*Monumental decision? Change your mind? Wait just a frog's ribbit. What did I just barge in on here? You weren't just about to…*

Leo's gasp had me swinging my gaze to the top of the files in the other chair. Of course, I couldn't see him. His horror at quickly figuring out what was taking place was ruining this moment.

*What moment? The one where you decided it would be better if we lived as toads? I don't want to be a toad! I've told you that a million times! You do realize that we'd have to live with warts for the rest of our lives, because that is what's going to happen if you spill the proverbial beans. The coven let the Heidi thing slide with only a warning, but the town sheriff? Oh, I feel an epic hairball coming up.*

Liam had begun to cautiously look in the direction of the other chair, his fingers squeezing mine in reassurance.

*I've decided that dying from heatstroke is more preferable to— what in sweet heaven is that thing doing here?*

Leo must have noticed the broomstick lying across Liam's desk. His gasp was even longer and louder than the previous one. I squeezed Liam's hand back, but not in reassurance. I was actually holding on for dear life.

*I leave for one hour, and you somehow figure out multiple ways to kill me off?*

There were times in life when the stress of it all became too much. This was one of those times, and my admission bubbled forth the same way it had when Heidi had walked in on me casting a spell in my living room.

*I'd hate to see what you come up with if you were truly trying.*

"I'm..."

*Don't...*

"A..."

*You...*

"Witch."

Leo didn't finish his warning, and I'm pretty sure the thud I heard was him hitting the ground.

# Chapter Nine

ONCE AGAIN, MY gaze kept sliding from where Leo most likely had landed in a heap in front of the desk back to where Liam knelt before me. There was literally no expression on his face, and I began to suspect he believed he'd misunderstood me.

Neither one of them had a said a word since my confession.

The temperature had risen another couple of degrees. At least, I'm pretty sure that was the reason I'd begun to break out in a fit of perspiration in some unspeakable places.

I'd have thought that the weight of such a secret taken off my shoulders would have been a huge relief. Instead, I was beginning to wonder if Liam had a paper bag stashed away somewhere in his desk. I was going to need it before I started to hyperventilate.

"I was expecting you to reveal you were a psychic or something, so you'll have to give me a minute here." Liam patted my hand like he would some confused elderly woman before he stood, only taking a step back so he could lean against his desk. He ran a hand over his face and spoke before I could ask him why on earth he would have thought I was a psychic. "You're not talking about simple holistic remedies, are you?"

I shook my head, still waiting rather impatiently for Leo to give me a sign that he hadn't perished from a heart attack.

A psychic? I'd suspected for quite a while that Liam had an idea that all was not normal in my world. There were times that I'd catch a sideways awkward glance my way over something I said or I'd find him beginning to ask me something before changing his mind and remaining quiet. But a psychic?

"All these months," Liam began before shaking his head in disbelief one more time. He hadn't picked up the phone yet. That was a good sign, right? "You somehow knew things that you had no way of knowing or gave me information about a case that you couldn't possibly have guessed. I chalked it up to coincidence the first and second time, but I was fairly positive I'd nailed it down by the time I drove you up to Windsor to look for your mother's sugar gliders."

I recalled that little road trip a bit too vividly, because that was when it had been revealed that Aunt Rowena was leading a faction against the other members of the council. It was selfish of me to hope the two factions were so busy with one another that they simply discarded my crime against the coven's rules.

Leo and I had gone over that little issue many times, because we weren't actually a part of the coven anymore. I figured the council just had more important matters to deal with than the Marigolds. We had been excommunicated long ago, and we didn't need to follow their policies or guidance. I also understood that the supernatural secret wasn't only mine to keep, but I'd disregarded their wisdom and told Heidi right out of the gate. That bit of insight, though, had been what was holding me back from letting Liam fully into my life. At what point was it worth sacrificing one's existence?

I had to clear my throat twice before I could speak.

"I'm not a psychic," I finally replied, trying to give Liam a smile of reassurance. I'm pretty sure I utterly failed. Would he have been more comfortable with me being a psychic than a witch? "I can cast divination spells to garner information when it's needed, harness energy from the earth to protect myself and those I love, and utilize magic to help others…though I can't use witchcraft for self-gain. It's a moral imperative."

"Magic spells?"

I slowly nodded, having come to the conclusion that Liam was definitely on the fence with how this conversation would pan out. If he could accept me as a psychic, there was no reason why he couldn't accept me as a witch. I just somehow needed to prove that itsy-bitsy detail to him.

"Leo, show yourself right now," I directed in a bit of desperation. Leo might have belonged to Nan in a past life, but I wouldn't want any other familiar than him. He was my partner in crime and in witchcraft. He was also the only proof I had at my disposal at the moment, because casting any type of spell with lightning overhead was a really bad idea. It was hard enough for me to control my own power, but adding the additional energy of a lightning storm I couldn't control was downright dangerous. That was truly a recipe for disaster. "Please, Leo. For both our sakes."

I'd seen Liam move fast before when pursuing a suspect, but I don't believe I've ever seen both of his boots come off the ground at the same time. One second he was in front of the desk, and the next moment he was two feet away to the side of it.

Leo had suddenly appeared right where I'd thought he'd be, with all four legs spread out on the old carpet from where he'd landed with a thud. He undeniably looked a bit worse for wear, and a part of me felt guilty for everything I'd put him through since figuring out my place in this life.

"Thank you," I murmured, knowing how much Leo had

been against confronting this very spectacle. My heart filled with love, and I patted my lap. No matter what happened in this moment, Leo would always be with me. "Thank you so much."

*Like I had any real choice. It was me either confirming your story or me watching the men in the white jackets drag you off in a padded white van. Don't believe for a second I didn't weigh my options, though. This is going to cost us both more than you know.*

I chuckled and pulled Leo close to me in a hug. The cool air that had remained inside the station had definitely begun to dissipate, leaving a building humidity that would likely leave us snapping at one another. Until that moment though, I didn't mind Leo's cat hairs sticking to my skin.

*It'll be warts by the time the council is done with us.*

The relief that this moment had finally arrived was very liberating, even with the threat of the council members looming over our lives. I'd stood up to them before, and I could do it again if need be. Plus, there was no reason why they even had to know I'd confided in Liam.

*I like the way you're thinking…for once. You can try making a habit out of this, you know. I wouldn't mind at all if you started keeping a few more of your more serious mistakes a secret. In the meantime, the good ol' sheriff seems to be a bit speechless.*

Liam was holding up a finger, as if to tell me to pause this current situation we'd found ourselves in. He was right. He hadn't planned to tell me he was falling in love with me during a power outage, and the same went for my sudden confession of witchcraft.

Well, timing wasn't exactly everything.

With the cursed broomstick now in my line of vision, it was time I put aside all doubt. I mean, really. What was so different between psychics and witches, anyway? Well, besides a familiar who'd been kept alive for a second go-round by a necromancy spell. It wasn't like no one had ever heard of a witch before. Well, in a general sort of way.

*Please don't put that on my tombstone. I'd prefer something a little more poetic.*

"I'm a witch, Leo is my familiar, and you have in your possession a broomstick that is actually cursed," I blurted out, standing up from the chair after Leo had hopped down to the floor. It didn't escape my notice that he'd backed up by a good three feet so that he wasn't the closest individual to the broomstick. "Liam…"

I raised my hand and covered his fingers with my own until his arm lowered to his side. He was still staring at Leo as if he was going to spontaneously combust, leaving behind a fiery cloud of a thousand smoldering cat hairs.

"Magic," I whispered, releasing my hold on Liam so that he had a bit of space to digest everything being thrown his way. "Liam, magic exists. The supernatural realm exists alongside you every single day. Nan used the tea shop to sell holistic tea blends, but those remedies had a touch of healing properties that the contents had nothing to do with. How do you think Otis gets around so well with his arthritis? Let's face it. Remission isn't something arthritis is normally known for, right? How do you think Wilma and Elsie bounce back so quick after catching a cold? It's not bee pollen extract. It's magic."

"Magic." Liam swallowed hard before pointing toward Leo. "And that?"

*Did the good ol' sheriff really just refer to me as an inanimate object?*

"That appearing out of nowhere thing?" Liam clarified, much to my relief. It wouldn't do him any good to have Leo on his bad side. "That's more than a magic trick, Raven."

"There are a lot of things in the supernatural realm that you might have a hard time believing in. Some things are true whether you believe in them or not. I'd love to take the time to tell you about all of them, if you want to hear about a few of your misconceptions, but right now...well, that broomstick might be the very thing that killed Sheriff O'Leary."

*About that...*

"Oh, Leo," I replied with a bit of desperation. "Please don't tell me that Aunt Rowena wasn't any help, because right now we need all the help we can get."

"What are you doing?" Liam asked, still observing Leo as if he would turn into a mountain lion right before our very eyes. "Are you really talking to him?"

*Now might be a good time to reconsider that memory erasing spell. You know, just in case the good ol' sheriff decides that he's gone over the deep end.*

"I can hear Leo's thoughts, yes."

I wasn't particularly liking the horrified expression on Liam's handsome face, either, but I wasn't about to lose hope. He'd adjust to my abilities, especially after he had all but expressed his love for me.

*How could you have turned out to be such a hopeless romantic after being raised by such a—*

"Leave Mom out of this," I chastised, understanding that Liam could only hear one side of the conversation. I could see how that might be a bit discerning. "Leo is my familiar. I can hear every thought he has and vice versa."

What I really wanted to be doing more than anything in the world was reciprocating Liam's declaration of love. Well, falling in love. I guess there was a difference, but it was still a step in the right direction.

*I'm pretty sure you just took two huge steps backward. And by two, I mean at least two miles' worth. Maybe more.*

"Heidi knows about my family's proclivities, too," I offered up, hoping that Liam would realize he had another human to talk to about all the things he was currently questioning. "She's the only one, because it's against coven rules to spill our secrets to the human realm. Not that my family belongs to a coven anymore, but I don't have time to get into that right now. What I'm trying to say is that I'm risking everything by telling you the truth, and I never would have done so if I wasn't falling in love with you, too."

*I'm pretty sure I'm sensing the beginnings of a hairball. Please don't make me hack up a hairball in the sheriff's office. It would be considered bad taste.*

My unexpected declaration had definitely caught Liam by surprise, and to the point that he finally dragged his gaze away from Leo to look at me. I mean, really look at me. It was easy to decipher the disbelief, but I could also make out his internal struggle to accept every word I was saying as the truth.

"You..." Liam let his sentence fade, clearly deciding to choose his words a bit more carefully. I braced myself for his rejection while holding out hope that he would accept me for...well, me. "I don't think there is any other woman in the world who can continue to surprise me on every level like you do almost every time we see one another."

*He has no idea...*

"Is that a good thing?" I asked, though I could barely hear the words myself.

*I'm putting this out there just for general information, but I really don't like being a third wheel.*

"Do it again," Liam directed unexpectedly, motioning with his hand that he wanted Leo to disappear. "Vanish and come back."

*What am I? A dog who performs those idiotic tricks? You tell that—*

"Leo," I prodded affectionately, observing Liam very closely to try and understand what he was truly looking for. "Please."

*Do I get my own bag of ice after we go to the gas station?*

"Yes."

*Fine. This will cost you, though. The minute we have electricity, I'm using your laptop to order that new Kiwi hydroponic catnip...it comes from New Zealand.*

"Done."

I was willing to agree to just about anything to grant Liam his request. Relief washed through me when Leo did his vanishing act, reappearing in record time.

*I just realized I'm no better than a dog jumping through hoops. They perform for treats. I perform for mental health necessities. There's something wrong with this equation.*

"That's..." Liam once again let his sentence trail off as he searched for the right words. "Incredible."

*That's the best he can do? The good ol' sheriff just witnessed a cat vanish into thin air. The best he can do is* incredible? *Raven, I'm beginning to suspect he's not the brightest bulb in the box.*

I was completely shocked when Liam pulled me into his arms, embracing me like I'd always imagined he would upon sharing our love for another. Granted, I'd put a hitch in that fantasy, but he was still following through with my best hopes for how this might turn out.

"I just needed to be sure that I wasn't losing my mind," Liam murmured against my ear, holding me even tighter against him.

We stayed that way until the temperature rose another degree and Leo had gone through his reasoning of why the New Zealand catnip might be more beneficial to his memory issue than the premium catnip from Honduras. I was now armed with more information about the minty herb than I'd ever wanted to be, but there were actually spells that utilized the tasty kitty treat.

"You didn't kick me out of the police station or call the looney bin," I said with hope, finally pulling away enough to give my body heat a chance to escape. "Does this mean you're willing to hear me out?"

Liam gently placed his palms on both sides of my cheeks, cradling my face tenderly.

"I'm not that easy to scare off, although for a brief moment I thought I was hallucinating." Liam pressed his forehead to mine. "I meant what I said, Raven. I fall more in love with you every single day, and something as small as discovering that witchcraft is real isn't going to change my mind about us."

*Wait until he hears that the local librarian is a werewolf with two mini-mes.*

"Thank you," I whispered, not knowing how else to show my gratitude that Liam was willing to have an open mind. I wrapped my arms around his neck and pulled him close one more time despite the heat. "Thank you for believing in me."

"In us, Raven," Liam corrected, tucking me in close.

He didn't seem to mind holding onto me a little while longer.

*Not to break up this romantic moment where we're likely to boil to death and melt into a pile of goo onto the floor, but we have more pressing issues. Not to say that you outing us to another human being isn't an important issue, because I'm pretty sure I can feel warts popping up on my skin underneath my fur. Regardless, I must now drop a huge bomb on your lovefest.*

"Leo, what are you talking about?" I asked, ever so slowly pulling away from Liam's embrace.

"This is going to take some getting used to," Liam muttered, setting his wary gaze on Leo. "What's he saying?"

*Tell the good ol' sheriff that if he starts to ask that question every ten seconds, we'll all be old and decrepit toads before I get the story out.*

"I sent Leo up to Windsor to find out more about the broomstick. Anyone in possession of the hexed broomstick dies within a specific timeframe. Unfortunately, we're not quite sure how long that is," I quickly explained, knowing that it wouldn't nearly be enough for my lawman. "Long story short, Mom buried it for safekeeping when she was a teenager after researching the object in question for a research paper. Mom is the reason we are currently in another blackout, because she used magic to discover who dug up the broomstick, which just so happened to be Sheriff O'Leary's deputy. So, I sent Leo up to Windsor to find out more about the curse so that we would be better prepared on how to dispose of the broomstick."

*That's the problem.*

"Leo, what do you mean that's the problem?" I asked, bracing myself for his answer. Sometimes, I think he enjoyed these moments a little too much. "What did Aunt Rowena say about the curse?

*Rowena has never heard of this so-called cursed broomstick nor anything other similar object being in the Barnes family's possession. Not a word, a peep, or a squeak. That can only mean one thing— we have no case and can now resume our regular, everyday lives! Hallelujah!*

# Chapter Ten

"YOU'VE BEEN INVOLVED in almost every case I've handled since you arrived in town, and that includes the investigations I've handed off to the state police." Liam held my hand as we both made our way across the scalding hot cobblestones of the crosswalk. I'd taken the additional time it took for the thunderstorm to pass, explaining what little I knew about the broomstick. We now had a plan in place, with the promise that we'd sit down when this murder mystery was solved to talk about us, in light of our circumstances as they were. That particular discussion would take longer than the thirty-three minutes we'd hunkered down in his office at the station. "Don't confirm that just yet."

Liam used to endearingly say that I ended up in the most precarious situations. I'd have been more stressed about the fallout of my confession if he hadn't been holding onto my hand so desperately.

Honestly, I didn't want to let go of him right now, either.

*You're causing me to perpetually choke on my tongue down here. Can you give it a break? This is no way for me to continue to live…with a witch who can't keep her sappy thoughts to herself. I'll have to double up on my intake of catnip. They say it helps with nausea, you know.*

"Leo, please go tell Mom to fix this power outage right

now," I muttered as we stepped onto the sidewalk. I didn't miss the way Liam darted his gaze around us to see if he could locate Leo. "It looks as if another storm is coming in off the bay, and it would be nice to have the power back on before it hits."

*What power outage? Boy, it's hot today, isn't it?*

"Leo, now is not the time for one of your short-term memory blips."

*What I've forgotten can't be that bad. You're holding hands with the good ol' sheriff. Are you two going to the malt shop for ice cream? That's a good idea, but I think I'll stick with whatever catnip treat Beetle brought into the shop today. I need to be on the top of my game if I'm going to locate Skippy and his band of ninja squirrels. They need to be dealt with.*

"Short-term memory blip?" Liam asked about ten feet from the antique shop's door. There was a chance that Kathleen had closed up the store, either due to her brother-in-law's murder or the fact that Paramour Bay still had no power. "Do I want to know?"

"You wouldn't have asked if you didn't," I replied with a smile, because I could hear the curiosity in his tone. However, it wasn't the bad kind. It was sincere interest in me and nearly everything that had to do with me. "You really have no idea what a relief it is to have you know everything."

*What did you say? Sweet angel of mercy, no wonder I didn't want to remember anything from the past hour, day, or week! My lord, what day is it? Holy moly, Batgirl! I feel an asthma attack coming on. It's not due to this horrendous heat, either. You still have Dr. Jameson on speed dial, right? I can't feel my paws.*

On the bright side, Leo's brain was reconnecting the dots. On the bad side, there was a closed sign hanging inside the door that brought Liam and I up short.

"Are you up for a road trip?"

*Depends. Does his truck have air conditioning that works better than the wish air you've got in your car? You know, like "I wish our air conditioning worked at full blast".*

Liam's question came out of nowhere, but it was also the best thing Liam could have asked me right now. It was a sign of blind trust.

*I think you're stretching his intent a bit, but the good ol' sheriff seems to be handling this well. You're not in cuffs. Hey, did you know that there is a spell to prevent someone from spilling secrets? You should learn the verbal component. Hey, just in case that doesn't work out, I'll see if I can find the right size hammer. One can never be too careful when a coven's council is one spell away from turning us into amphibians. Back to this air conditioning issue...*

"You mean, a road trip to talk to Kathleen and her sister?"

*Wrong question. First, air conditioning. Then your silly case. Do you need me to spell that out for you?*

"Yes," Liam replied, already turning on his boots and using his free hand to pull out the keys to his truck. "Jack gives me leeway on the cases that I hand over to him. We've always worked well together, and we already know that Lydia was the one to tell Jack about the curse. I assume Kathleen is aware of it, too. We can say that your grandmother knew the Barnes family, and that nothing of the kind was ever said in passing. It will give us an excuse to ask a few more questions about why Sheriff O'Leary had a list of herbal poisons in his hand when he died."

"Wouldn't Jack have already asked Kathleen or Lydia about the list?"

*Again, wrong question. My fur is beginning to knot in places it shouldn't due to the humidity factor. It's spelled like this—A- I- R- C...*

"Jack did inquire about the note, but Lydia stated she didn't know anything about it." Liam pressed a button on his key fob, bringing the engine to life as Leo continued to spell out his fantasy. Liam opened up the passenger side door and saw to it that I was settled comfortably in the seat. He did a double take when Leo materialized right on top of the middle console. "I'll be right back. I just need to forward the phone lines to my cell."

*Point those two middle vents right toward me. That's right. A little to the left on that one and…ahhhhh. Perfect. A bit warm, but this newer model will no doubt spit cool air out faster than your death trap's tired old compressor.*

"That went better than I expected, Leo," I murmured, watching Liam jog back into the station.

My admiration for the man spiked considerably, given that he was the type of male who liked cold, hard facts. You know, things that fit into an established mold. Granted, Leo had been able to provide proof, but I had an intuition that Liam would have put his faith in me, regardless. The t-shirt that he was wearing instead of his usual button down khaki dress shirt framed his biceps just right. As the door closed behind him, I couldn't help but admire the way his denim jeans—

*Raven Lattice Marigold! Get your mind out of the gutter right this minute. I swear, listening to your twisted thoughts might be worse than enduring this horrendous heat wave. Speaking of which, can you adjust that other vent half a degree more toward me? You're not the one wearing a fur coat here.*

Liam quickly returned, settling in behind the steering wheel. He didn't say a word about the fact that Leo had all but claimed both the vents on the middle console and had his crooked whiskers tilted toward the roof of the cab so that the cool air hit him directly in the neck. Instead, Liam just shifted the gear into drive and made a U-turn to head toward the highway.

*He's got promise, but I still don't think the good ol' sheriff was worth being turned into a French side dish...frog legs a la crispy. Hey, ask where he bought this truck, will ya? You need to get rid of that death trap, and his air conditioning is top notch. I'm might actually be getting frostbite.*

"I have a lot of questions running through my mind," Liam said, and not for the first time in the last hour. I'd basically given a crash course regarding my life since coming to Paramour Bay, but the details had been vague. It was best for me to ease him into my daily existence. "I agree that O'Leary's murder needs to be cleared up first, though. Start from the beginning on only those specific details having to do with the...cursed broomstick."

"Well, I didn't know it was truly cursed until Heidi called yesterday. She knew about my visit with Mazie and Lucille, so—"

"Lucille? As in Lucille Rebecca Barnes? Jack mentioned that the myth regarding the broomstick was from centuries ago." Liam shot me a confused glance. "Jack pulled up her descendants in one of the databases, thinking maybe the broomstick was some sort of antique that was worth money. That alone could be a motive for murder. Jack has a few relatives to check out, but I don't believe there was a Lucille on the list."

*Have I mentioned my love for front row seats? I can't wait for you to tell him about our surprise visit from the afterlife. You don't happen to have any catnip on you, do you? This is why you need to start carrying around a purse like Heidi. She gets me. I could use my pipe right about now.*

I ran the palms of my hands down the fabric of my skirt. I'd already thrown quite a bit at him, but explaining that spirits could actually walk among us might be more than he could handle.

"When you say visit, you're not talking about it being in person, are you?"

*Smarter than the average bear. That's good to know. He's intuitive.*

"Um, do you recall when you drove my mother and I up to Windsor regarding her pet sugar gliders?"

*You're really going to throw the good ol' sheriff into the deep end, aren't you? No life preserver, no easing him into the shallow end. Just drown the poor guy and be done with it.*

"That trip was hard to forget," Liam said somewhat wryly, having already mentioned that was the moment he realized something more was going on with me than met the eye.

*Tell me about it. I still have Strifle's fairy glitter stuck to my fur. You'd think it would have turned to goo in this heat, but noooo…it just stays stuck there in my fur, mocking me.*

"Technically, there were no sugar gliders," I admitted, thinking back to my run-in with the council. "Mazie had already passed through the veil, but her familiar had been held back from crossing over by dark magic. She came to me asking if I'd help figure out who would do such a thing, and all leads pointed toward the coven. But Mazie wasn't alone. Lucille had escorted her back through the veil for our little tea party."

"The veil?" Liam reiterated, though his was more of an inquiry. His thumb drummed on the steering wheel a little harder than usual. "Spirits. They came to visit you. Real ghosts."

*That was some shove, Raven. Swim, big boy. Swim.*

I shot Leo a sideways glance, but his eyes were closed, almost as if he was relishing this moment. It didn't help that he had a Cheshire grin plastered underneath his crooked whiskers.

"Maybe Aunt Rowena was right about the broomstick not being cursed. Had there been such an item, I'm sure the council members would have been tempted to retrieve such a powerful object." It was best to gloss right over the spirit part of this equation. "Leo explained to me how hard it was to enchant a random item. Believe me, it's harder than just throwing some material components in a pestle and reciting a few special words."

I'm almost certain Liam just muttered underneath his breath about finally understanding why the shop and my cottage had so many pestles and mortars. At least he wasn't still focused on the spirit world.

*What a fuddy-duddy. You're not making the trip enjoyable in the least bit.*

"Has Jack spoken to Sheriff O'Leary's deputy?" I asked, wanting to know how he knew there was a broomstick to dig up in the first place. "Who told him about the broomstick?"

"The deputy's name is Roger Wilson." Liam flipped his turn signal on as we reached the ramp to the highway. He was now in his element while talking about the facts of the case. "Wilson claims he was hiking on his day off. He tripped over something, realized that it wasn't a tree root, and then decided to dig whatever it was up that was sticking out of the ground."

Liam gracefully merged his truck onto the highway, leaving me to wonder where the broomstick fit into this murder mystery.

*It could just be a coinkydink. That would be in our favor, you know what I mean?*

"You mean coincidence," I corrected while still wondering about the list of herbal plants that could be used to poison a person. "Did Jack ever find out why Sheriff O'Leary had that list of herbal poisons in his hand?"

*You really need to brush up on your urban dictionary, Raven. A coinkydink is a coincidence. It's just the new hip way of saying it. Get with the program, square.*

"Jack is going over open cases with Deputy Wilson, hoping one sheds some light on where Sheriff O'Leary may have come up with that list." Liam thinned his lips as he set the speed control to a few miles above the posted sign. "If it turns out there was a death recently where the sheriff suspected poison, it's a safe bet that his own murder is tied to that case."

*That would leave witchcraft off the weapon list, as well as your mother getting her research wrong all those years ago. A double win for our team. With this cool air blowing in my face, I'd say it's a trifecta.*

I couldn't help but observe the gathering storm clouds to my left. The palm of my right hand had been tingling ever since we'd started this journey north. Leo might believe that witchcraft wasn't involved, but everything inside of me was all but screaming that the broomstick and list of herbal poisons were connected in some way.

*You're such a buzzkill. Remind me not to take you to the track.*

# Chapter Eleven

"OKAY," LIAM STATED with determination after finally exiting his truck and walking around to the front where I was waiting for him. "I just got off the radio with Jack. He's with Deputy Wilson right now. They are going over his initial statement."

We'd arrived at Deidre O'Leary's residence to find quite a few vehicles in the driveway. This probably wasn't the best time to stop in, but I was thinking like an amateur sleuth. Liam was law enforcement, and it was his job to find out who had poisoned Sheriff O'Leary.

*It could very well have been an accident. Stakeouts can be rough, all those endless hours sitting by himself in a vehicle. Who knows what he had to resort to in order to stay awake to apprehend the unsub.*

"Uh, where did Leo go?" Liam asked, seeming a bit anxious as he looked around the property. It was beautiful land, too. Sheriff O'Leary and his wife hadn't lived in town, but rather on the outskirts. I hadn't realized small town sheriffs made so much, because this homestead with its acres of land had to run somewhere in the seven figures. "I was going to leave the truck running with the air conditioning on while we spoke with Mrs. O'Leary."

*I never know how to act when the good ol' sheriff puts me above taxpayers' expense. I'm pretty sure that means you don't go out of your way often enough.*

"Leo is right beside us, talking like he's in some Sam Spade novel and commenting needlessly on every little thing," I muttered, walking by Liam's side as we made our way toward the front door. Wraparound porches were more my thing, but this type of house wasn't built with the country vibe in mind. The two white pillars were huge. It gave me more of the plantation vibe. "I'm wondering if I shouldn't be the one to stay behind in the truck. How are you going to explain my presence?"

*I ask myself that very question every time you get us involved with one of these escapades.*

"Easy," Liam responded, taking time to survey the sky above us. The storm that had been coming across the bay had no doubt already hit our town. There was a good chance we would catch the edge of the storm as it continued east. "The autopsy hasn't been completed yet, and you're known around Paramour Bay for your expertise in herbal extracts. I'm going to say that I brought you along as my Subject Matter Expert, better known as SME."

*Expert might be stretching it a bit. You might want to stick to the truth about being a student of herbal supplements. Hey, do you suppose Deidre O'Leary is a witch, too? The name Deidre just conjures up some wacky spells being cast over a cauldron.*

It had crossed my mind that someone close to the sheriff might be a witch or a wizard, especially given the fact that he had the cursed broomstick in his possession.

*Just say broomstick. We don't know if it's actually hexed. I told you, that takes a great deal of time and effort. Your mother tried it once during her childhood, and that was an utter failure. We never covered that subject again.*

With the way this case was turning out, I wasn't sure I even wanted to cover that lesson myself.

"It's not like I can go searching through the house for poisonous herbs and plants," I whispered, afraid someone would overhear me since he'd already rang the doorbell.

"Can't you…" Liam tilted his head a few times to indicate witchcraft. "You know, wiggle your nose or something?"

*Does he have a facial tic? The good ol' sheriff should really get that checked out.*

"It's not that easy," I managed to reply before the front door swung open.

*Jackpot.*

I recognized the blonde woman immediately as Kathleen Reynolds, the antique store owner and sister of Deidre O'Leary. We'd never met personally, as her assistant at the shop was more hands-on with the customers. I liked Lydia.

*Suspect number one. Seeing as the good ol' sheriff is still trying to adjust to your confession and you're stuck on some clue about a curse that might not exist, that leaves me to figure out who poisoned the neighboring sheriff. This is bound to cause my memory issues to worsen, isn't it?*

"Liam," Kathleen exclaimed with a mixture of relief and something else that came across as anxiety. She was quite tiny, standing probably at five feet, two inches. Her lack of height didn't make her any less elegant. She wore a black dress with a lot of silver jewelry that was definitely from a different era. Her frown was evident when her gaze landed on me. "Raven Marigold?"

*It's rude to keep us out here on the front porch in this heat. Did you hear that rumbling of thunder? Either that was from the storm or your mother is attempting to fix her atypical blunder when it comes to casting elemental spells. That's a sign, you know. Your mother has only ever flubbed up casting twice by my count before she supposedly gave up the witchcraft way of life. I'd be more than happy to tell you about them, but the details escape me.*

"Hi, Kathleen," Liam greeted the antique shop owner with a sympathetic smile. "I know we spoke at length yesterday, but I'm helping Detective Swanson with the investigation. Is it alright if we come in for a moment?"

*At least we know that Kathleen isn't heartless the way Purple Pearl portrayed her to be this morning. She's here with her sister, so that counts for something, right?*

"Of course, of course," Kathleen agreed, stepping back on the marble floor. The coolness of the interior was an immediate relief, and I could hear Leo sigh with happiness when he'd followed suit. "Deidre is in the sitting room with a couple of her close friends."

*The connotation she used on the word friends makes it sound like we're about to venture into a pit of vipers. I might just stay right where I am…soaking up the cold from these spectacular marble tiles. Is there a reason we don't have these at the cottage? They would have come in handy during the blackout.*

"Could we have a moment of your time before we join them?" Liam asked, waiting for Kathleen to face us. She really was a beautiful woman, and I guessed she was somewhere in her mid-fifties. "I'd like to ask you a few more questions about why Sheriff O'Leary came to see you yesterday."

Kathleen inhaled deeply and tilted her chin in such a fashion one would think she was getting ready to do battle. She wasn't acting like a guilty party, but it was easy to get the sense that she was withholding information. The palm of my hand had begun to tingle more than ever since we'd been granted access to this house.

*You're going to make me leave this wonderful foyer, aren't you? This marble is so smooth and shiny and cool and…*

I shifted to the right just a bit, knowing full well that Leo had all but collapsed onto the marble. It wasn't as if we hadn't spent an hour inside an air-conditioned vehicle. One would think he was still back in Paramour Bay with my mother sweating out the storm.

*You need to take lessons in caretaking from the good ol' sheriff. At least he offered to let me stay in the truck instead of…*

I could literally hear Leo sniffing the air.

*Is that catnip I smell?*

There was no question in my mind that Leo had skedaddled into the other room as fast as he could waddle, not waiting for me to direct him toward the kitchen where some poisonous herbs might be stored in the pantry. The experts always say that the spouse was usually the guilty party in these kinds of cases, so it's a fair assumption that Deidre might very well have a motive for killing her husband—money or possibly infidelity.

*Was that chandelier made of diamonds?*

"I wasn't at the shop yesterday when Pat paid me a visit," Kathleen said, sticking to her original statement. "My assistant, Lydia, called me immediately when she saw all the commotion outside and realized that Pat had…"

Kathleen cleared her throat, obviously overcome with grief.

"Lydia told Detective Swanson that Pat stopped into the store to see if we knew anything regarding an old broomstick. Either Pat was working some kind of case or he wanted to see if the broomstick in question was an antique of sorts. Deidre collects odd knickknacks and such, though she's usually more serious about her discoveries." Kathleen gently wrapped her small fingers around the bracelets hanging from her wrist. "I'm not that particular. I love all things that have some history attached to them."

It was clear that Kathleen loved and cherished the items that came into her shop. This was usually where Leo would pipe in and claim that the least suspicious person—in this case, Kathleen—was the guilty party.

I sure hoped Leo was somewhere in the kitchen looking for some poisonous herbs or somewhere on the property in search of a greenhouse. Catnip had a way of detouring him from his assigned tasks, much like Liam and coffee did for me.

"Detective Swanson mentioned that Lydia told Sheriff O'Leary about a curse associated with the broomstick," Liam prodded, giving Kathleen the impression that he wasn't buying something like that. Oh, he was good. Really good. For reference, I was a horrible liar. "Why would Lydia have told the sheriff an old myth like that?"

"Because it's true, Liam," Kathleen replied with earnest and a small smile. She waved a hand toward an ornate vase that was filled with different sized reeds on a thin table against the far wall of the foyer. "It is said that this particular antique has healing properties. The painting hanging above the vase is said to bring prosperity."

One out of two wasn't too bad, but I wasn't going to say that aloud.

"Lydia is really into the occult, which is why we have a section of the shop for items such as tarot cards, Ouija boards, voodoo dolls, and that kind of supernatural stuff," Kathleen responded in a manner which spoke volumes to the entrepreneur side of things.

The interest in things that people can't explain was like a magnet. It did make me wonder just which residents might buy into those objects, and if there were any real truth to some of the stories attached to them. It was something I'd have to run by Leo, if he ever returned from his scavenger hunt.

"And Lydia somehow recognized the broomstick?" Liam asked, still digging for some type of answer as to how she had known about the hex. "Out of the blue?"

Hearing about the small section of the shop that contained occult items had me wanting to peruse what content they had, with Leo by my side, of course. If there were any dangerous items on the shelves, it would be better if I could purchase them and store them away in a safe and guarded place where no would could reach them.

"My heavens, no." Kathleen's light chuckle echoed around the foyer. "Lydia had to search the internet, but she finally found a paranormal phenomenon website that explained the lineage of the broomstick, although no one quite knows all the details. You see, the letter B that was branded on the handle belonged to the Barnes family. I believe they used to reside up near Windsor, but their relatives are now scattered all over the globe. Somewhere along the way a curse began to be associated with the broomstick, although there was no clear reason other than a few deaths in the Barnes descendants."

My mother had seemed pretty adamant about the curse, but what if the broomstick actually *had* simply been a chestnut handle with birch twigs on the end? At this point, I wasn't sure about anything.

"Do you believe the curse had anything to do with your brother-in-law's death?" Liam continued to question Kathleen, even though Deidre had emerged from the sitting room. I'm not sure how I expected her to appear, but she seemed even more poised than her sister. Not a tear streak could be found in the woman's makeup, and her mascara looked to have been expertly applied by an artist. "And did Sheriff O'Leary mention a list of herbs or plants to Lydia?"

"Not that I recall," Kathleen answered, stepping to the side so that her sister could join us. "Deidre, you remember Sheriff Liam Drake. And this is Raven Marigold. She owns the tea shop in Paramour Bay."

"How may we help you?" Deidre asked, not wasting any time. She had a white handkerchief in her hand with the initials *RCW* embroidered on one corner. "Have you or Detective Swanson found the monster who murdered my husband?"

*Wow. I'm gone for five minutes, and you've managed to whip the widow into a fury. Don't let her fool you. She's a horrible person, Raven. Horrible. You should see the pathetic generic catnip she gives her tabby. It was almost not worth consuming. I doubt it cost five cents an ounce, and these people could buy all the catnip farms in Honduras, just like I've always dreamed—a catnip plantation of my very own, with plenty of staff to serve my every need.*

"Detective Swanson is following up on leads as we speak, but I was hoping that we could ask you and your friends a few questions."

*You'll want to focus on the blonde and the brunette on the couch. While I was passing through the sitting room, they were whispering to each other something fierce. I'd hoped it was a coup against the way this redhead treats her tabby, but all I caught was something about hiding the evidence.*

Evidence? Had it been that easy to catch the killer? In this case, killers? Leo simply walking through the sitting room and accidentally hearing a confession would be a first.

*I could have hallucinated the whole thing. Who knows what they put in that generic catnip-like substance? It could be laced with something or—*

Leo's gasp of horror was unmistakable.

*Poisoned!*

"My friends?" Deidre inquired with a rather offended expression. There wasn't a strand of her red hair that was out of place. "Why on earth would you need to speak with my friends? I can assure you that no one in our inner circle could ever commit a crime, Sheriff Drake, let alone take my husband's life."

*Are you listening to me, Raven? Poison! Oh, no. I feel an asthma attack coming on. What if it's not due to stress, and has everything to do with me ingesting poison? Tell the good ol' sheriff that he needs to arrest this woman right now! Get her to confess so that I can die knowing justice has been served!*

Leo would continue to carry on hysterically unless I proved to him that the catnip hadn't been laced with poison. With that said, no one would ever catch me drinking anything under this roof without solid proof that Deidre didn't murder her husband.

*And that helps me how? I'm growing weaker by the minute, Raven.*

"It's just standard procedure, and you never know what your husband may have said to someone in passing that could provide us useful information," Liam explained, casting me a questioning glance when he realized that I wasn't really paying attention to the conversation at hand. I shrugged slightly, so that he'd know I was speaking with Leo. "I brought Raven with me due to the herbal components that were written down on a piece of paper we found at the scene."

Deidre gave a rather loud sigh, as if we were bothering her when we were only trying to find out who killed her husband. One would think she would be a little more grateful. As the sheriff's wife turned on her black heels, we slowly fell into step behind her.

*I can't take another step. My limbs are too weak.*

A tabby made an appearance, the black slits of her light green eyes practically slim lines as she zeroed in to the right side of my leg. She could sense Leo's presence and smell his scent. I'm surprised she waited so long to hiss and arch her back in protest, but she did so theatrically. On the bright side, the catnip couldn't be laced. The fact that the feline was alive was proof of that theory.

*Hmmmm. You have a good point. No wonder that tabby has such a bad attitude. Now I just feel sorry for her. Apparently, the generic catnip has affected her mental health.*

"Princess, stop that," Deidre chastised, causing her tabby to hiss once more before running into the sitting room to hide. "I apologize for my baby. She's been out of sorts since…"

Deidre couldn't seem to finish her sentence, and I wondered if maybe I hadn't read the situation wrong. After all, everyone grieved in different ways.

*I'm grieving for Princess. To be named so nobly like that and only be given generic catnip is a travesty. These people should be brought up on animal cruelty charges. Neglect of a dependent.*

"Ladies, if I could have your attention, please," Deidre interrupted in a very regal manner, causing the soft murmurs around the room to come to a halt. "This is Sheriff Drake from Paramour Bay, and he has some questions to ask us. Sheriff, Becca Wilson and Claire Wesley are the two women on the couch, and my other friend sitting in the chair is Laura Midleaf. I honestly don't know what I would have done without them."

*Did you see that look between those two women on the couch? They know something, Raven. Oh, and there were no herbs in the kitchen besides that generic plastic bottle of cheap catnip. Really. The nerve of these people.*

I had caught the way Becca had glanced at Claire, and it was an obvious expression of anxiety. I should know, because that was the exact look I had on my face when my mother told me about conducting a spell in the middle of a thunderstorm. But I'd made a connection that I really needed to convey to Liam, but there wasn't a chance I could do it discreetly without being overheard.

*Connection? What connection? I'm a little busy trying to stay alive over here, in case you hadn't noticed. Do something so that I don't die with the aftertaste of generic catnip on my tongue. Who would have thought heatstroke would have been a preferable way to go?*

Sure enough, Princess seemed to be circling the room with her wide gaze glued to where Leo remained invisible. I could only hope that she didn't draw attention to him.

"I'm sorry we have to meet under such circumstances," Liam began, stopping short when Kathleen offered both of us a beverage.

*Go back to this connection you think you've made. The sooner we wrap this up, the better. I think our not-so-sweet Princess has gone feral. You know, that happens when given generic catnip over a long time period, poor thing. She has succumbed to inferior pet care products.*

"Becca?" I inquired of the brunette, allowing Liam to answer Kathleen regarding our drinks. "Becca Wilson? Are you related to Deputy Wilson?"

I was particularly interested in Deidre's reaction, because she was the one who was currently holding Deputy Wilson's handkerchief. The white squared fabric could have easily been given to the grieving widow by Becca, or even by Deputy Wilson himself in a gentlemanly fashion when making a condolence call. By the way Deidre was clutching the embroidered handkerchief to her chest, I'd say the odds were against that theory.

*Ohhhhh, an old-fashioned love triangle gone bad story. We now have multiple suspects, although I still haven't ruled out not-so-sweet Princess' participation in this Machiavellian cabal. I'd be pushed to murder someone over the shredded cardboard pieces they sell as generic catnip. That's it, Raven! The dead sheriff wasn't killed because of the hexed broomstick, he was murdered by his cat!*

# Chapter Twelve

ONE HOUR LATER, Liam had finally obtained what little information he could uncover on the list of poisons that Sheriff O'Leary had clutched in his hand upon his death. What had been acquired was the story of how Deputy Wilson retrieved the broomstick…and it was nothing too miraculous. A simple trip over something buried in the woods led to the excavation of a hexed broomstick.

*I don't know about you, but I'm ready to take that broomstick and hit someone over the head with it if we don't get out of here within the next five minutes.*

It wasn't as if Leo had to worry about Princess anymore. Deidre had noticed her cat's odd behavior and taken her into the kitchen when she went to retrieve us two glasses of ice water. Kathleen had joined her, and everyone could make out the mumbled argument ensuing throughout the house. The two were barely speaking by the time they'd rejoined everyone in the living room.

*Not to get off topic here, but do you think that your mother has corrected her earlier faux pas? Is it too much to ask for a normal day at the tea shop where I get to lounge on my pillow in the display window while occasionally making fun of the residents as they pass by? We can make that happen, you know. There's a spell somewhere that erases the last twenty-four hours from everyone's memory. We've had this conversation many times...I think.*

Liam had filled in the awkward silence by asking Claire and Laura for when the last time they'd seen or spoken to Sheriff O'Leary. These couples played a card game called Euchre once a week on Wednesday, but it was Becca who had seen Sheriff O'Leary the morning of his death. It was time to come back around to that topic, and Liam was apparently on the same page with me.

"Becca, you mentioned that you were visiting your husband at the station yesterday morning," Liam directed his statement to the brunette while holding his phone at an odd angle. "Did Sheriff O'Leary act unusual or say anything out of the ordinary that you noticed?"

*Seriously? The good ol' sheriff is trying to get you to read a text message. Do I have to do everything around here? By the way, I'm starting to itch. I think it might be a side effect from that generic catnip.*

Liam and I were currently seated on the smaller sofa, so I leaned forward and pretended to adjust the hem of my skirt. The message was from Jack. It appeared that Deputy Wilson hadn't known that Sheriff O'Leary had a trip planned into Paramour Bay yesterday morning. The first time the deputy realized the sheriff had left the township's limits was from the subsequent phone call regarding the death of Sheriff O'Leary.

*I've got to be allergic to the generic variety. It's the only reasonable explanation as to why I'm itching like I've just rolled in a patch of poison ivy. Wait. Can cats even get poison ivy?*

"Pat had the broomstick that my husband discovered during his hiking trip," Becca revealed, though we'd already known that piece of information. "He mentioned that he was going to pay Kathleen a visit at her shop to see if she could give him any information on something so old, but Pat didn't say anything about herbs or plants."

I experienced a slight head rush when Becca's reply had me straightening up on the couch. She'd completely blown apart her husband's statement without even realizing what she'd done. Maybe my theory was wrong that Deidre and Roger Wilson were having an affair. What if Becca had mentioned hiding evidence for her husband? What if Roger Wilson had killed his boss? He was in the perfect position to cover up a crime, especially with his wife's help.

*I can't have whiplash on top of an allergic reaction. Stick with one theory at a time, would you?*

My phone vibrated, but I ignored the call. It was most likely Heidi, wondering what was going on in the investigation. If Jack was currently questioning Deputy Wilson, it was safe to assume that Heidi had been dropped back at her house. She was most likely wishing she were anywhere else now that the power had gone out again.

"Did you, by chance, hear Sheriff O'Leary discussing a case he might be investigating that involved herbs or plants of any sort?"

Whoever it was that wanted to get ahold of me was very persistent. My phone began to vibrate once more.

*Your mother. That's who is persistent, and she's also a thorn in my—*

"Excuse me," I mumbled, leaving Liam to finish his questioning right when we'd been given our first lead. It didn't take me long to make it to the foyer and pull out my phone. Sure enough, Leo was right about who was calling. "Mom, we're in the middle of something, so I'm going to have to call you back."

*Don't hang up! Sweet angel of mercy, don't hang up that phone!*

*Ask her if she fixed the power outage, and also let her know that we're on to her. Mention Rowena while I try and get rid of this itch on the back of my neck. It's enough to cause a cat to go insane.*

"You'll be happy to know that power has been restored, Beetle has reopened the tea shop, and our little broomstick problem has been taken care of," my mother announced with pride. I, on the other hand, wasn't sure how to react to the last matter she'd just declared. "You can thank me later. Oh, and the broomstick wasn't the cause of that poor sheriff's death. Isn't that reassuring? Now, seeing as I'm in town, I thought I might be able to shed some light on your current murder mystery. I'm about to walk into this quaint antique shop that is just darling. I hadn't realized that the store had changed hands since I'd moved away. I can't wait to see the charming antiques. Of course, I'll chat up the woman behind the register to see exactly what she and the sheriff discussed yesterday morning."

Lydia must have reopened the antique shop, but that's not what had me concerned.

*I've decided to let this allergic reaction be the cause of my oh-so-dramatic death. Leave me, dear Raven, to die in peace. I'm not sure if squirrels even know the pleasure of catnip, but make sure that Skippy gets my emergency rations that are hidden underneath my pillow in the display window. He's earned it with his tenacity and verve in his attempts to ruin my life, but in the end...I've always known my death would be at the hands of your mother.*

"Mom, don't you dare go in that store," I muttered fiercely, stepping closer to the front door so that no one inside the sitting room could hear my side of the conversation. "You have some explaining to do. Even Leo knows that you would never have risked casting a spell with a thunderstorm over the bay, and don't you dare say you didn't know lightning was near. Even I can sense when the elements around us change. Second, Leo went to speak with Aunt Rowena about Lucille Barnes' broomstick. Guess what? She said that she'd never heard of such a myth until recent years. Why is that? You said you were told all about the myth when you were a teenager, but that's not quite true, is it? What are you trying to cover up, Mom?"

*Really? Those are the two topics you focus on after she all but announced she somehow annihilated the broomstick in question? Priorities, Raven. Priorities.*

Honestly, I was hoping that Leo's short-term memory loss had affected mine. We had to have been mistaken about the annihilation part, as was often the problem when it came to my mother. The broomstick was safely locked up at the police station.

"Why on earth would you think I'm covering up something?"

*You realize that Regina hasn't said a word about Rowena, right? That alone is a giant red flag that your mother is guilty of something, most likely whatever this itch is underneath my fur. Ask that witch if she put a spell on me.*

"Talk, Mother," I demanded, wondering if I should call Heidi and suggest she send my mother back to the city. Having her in Paramour Bay on a mere visit was enough to send me to an early grave. "Now."

My mother's sigh of resignation was audible.

*Be on your guard, Raven. Your mother is a master manipulator, as proven by her relationship with my BFF. I still can't get those horrible images out of my head.*

"I stole the broomstick back, cast an itsy-bitsy spell to ensure that the curse wasn't responsible for that poor sheriff's death, and then reburied it in a place that no one would ever think to look."

*Can we just call it a week and start anew Monday? Seriously, I'm not so sure how things go from bad to worse and then to full-on-apocalypse mode without Skippy being responsible for world domination. Oh, that's right. We're talking about your mother, the queen of doom.*

"What do you mean that you stole the broomstick?"

It was better to begin my interrogation one question at a time, because I wasn't sure I'd be able to talk otherwise. Liam was currently getting some valuable information to help us solve this case, and I was missing the chance to ask my own questions about what herbs and plants the sheriff might have inadvertently ingested twenty-four hours prior to his death.

"Stole might be a tad bit of an exaggeration," my mother explained with a morsel of irritation, most likely getting aggravated by having to stand outside the antique shop in the heat. "I took back the cursed broomstick from the police station. It's in a safe place now, and you don't have to worry that Liam's life will be sacrificed to the curse. Wicked hex, that one. Now, can we please move on to another topic?"

*A master manipulator at her finest. Getting the truth out of your mother is like trying to get Ted to talk in complete sentences.*

"No, we cannot move on from the fact that you stole something right out of a police station." I hadn't realized I'd taken my phone away from my ear in order to be able to yell directly into the speaker on my phone. Okay, it wasn't so much of a yell as it was an angry whisper. "How am I going to explain that to Liam?"

*Don't bring up the good ol' sheriff or else your mother will know what you've done by spilling the witch beans, if you get my drift. Stay the course, Raven, while I use this table leg to try and scratch this itch.*

"I used a bit of magic to unlock the front door before care-fully taking the broomstick back to the cottage for an itsy-bitsy spell after the last storm cloud passed by overhead. Before you get yourself worked up into a frenzy, no one saw a thing," my mother reassured me, as if I was going to take her word for it after Aunt Rowena all but popped the balloon on the whole hex thing. "This murder mystery of yours is all on the up and up. No witchcraft attached to it in the least."

*You should look up the website that Lydia did for Sheriff O'Leary regarding hexed items. We're missing something, but this maddening itch won't let me think straight.*

"That doesn't make me feel better, Mom. You know firsthand the risk you took casting a spell on a cursed item." I heard the vase wobble behind me, and I managed to make it across the foyer and stabilize the ornate ceramic before Leo could knock it to the floor. A quick peek inside the sitting room showed that Liam was still deep in conversation with the women. "Go back to the tea shop. Whatever you do, do not cast any more spells or get yourself caught up in this murder investigation any more than you already have."

I disconnected the call before my mother could argue, agree-ing with Leo that we'd missed something very vital when it came to the broomstick. It was almost as if it were a red herring keeping us from knowing the truth about Sheriff O'Leary's murder.

"Leo, show yourself quick," I whispered, kneeling low on the marble floor. "I'll take a look and see what's bothering you."

Surprisingly, Leo materialized before I finished my sentence.

*Well? Scratch my back! Do something before my insanity reaches a whole other level of madness.*

"What is hanging from your mouth?" I asked, wiping a small

morsel of food from a tuft of hair. "Were you eating out of Princess' bowl?"

*Maybe.*

There was no hiding my smile, because whatever Leo had eaten out of Princess' bowl had most likely caused an allergic reaction. It hadn't been the catnip, but Leo had been on the right track about his hypersensitivities to certain food colorings. It was one of the reasons I stuck with the fresh natural ingredient cat food we purchased from an online website.

"Can you breathe okay?" I asked Leo, scratching the back of his neck to give him some relief from the reaction.

Leo's left eye bulged a bit, and his whiskers twitched twice.

*I don't know. I was, but now that you brought it up…well, I'm not sure. Am I wheezing? You realize that you're no help to me at all right now. I might as well have done an internet search on my symptoms. Did you know that hacking up a hairball leads to death? I should know, because I looked it up one time. Every symptom eventually leads to death if you follow the trail through the worldwide web, Raven. I'm a goner. This is it.*

"You're breathing just fine," I replied wryly, tousling his ears. He hated it, but it would get his mind off his itch. There were no other symptoms, but I would give Dr. Jameson's office a call to make sure I shouldn't give Leo some type of antihistamine. "Now, no more eating out of other cat's bowls."

I really wanted to join Liam and the others in the sitting room, but Leo's health was paramount above all else. A quick phone call revealed that I could give Leo an antihistamine, which meant a little bit of acting on my part. We were quite a drive from Paramour Bay, and I didn't want to wait that long before giving Leo some relief from his itching.

*The worst actress on the planet is going to try to pretend she has allergies to save my life. I already know the ending, so leave me to suffer in my last few minutes.*

"Don't be so dramatic," I chastised, knowing full well that I wouldn't have to pull something like this off by myself. Liam would step in once I was able to explain the situation, and he would see to it that Leo got his medication. "See? There are some major advantages to having Liam know our little secret."

*Death might be preferable than being turned into a toad by a council who can't even agree on the rules for their own coven.*

Leo had a point, but not about being turned into a frog. Sooner or later, the council would have to be dealt with. In the meantime, we had a murder to solve.

*And an antihistamine to track down! Do me a favor, though. I stand a better chance of survival with someone else at the helm...meaning the good ol' sheriff. The Marigold women—sans my precious Rosemary—have the worst time with directions.*

Leo didn't bother to say another word after I gave him a look of warning, so similar to my mother's famous arched brow. He disappeared in a puff of hair.

"Smart choice," I muttered, slipping my cell phone into my pocket as I stood from my kneeling position. "Remind me again who couldn't resist temptation, ended up eating out of another cat's bowl, and now has to contend with an allergic reaction?"

*Raven one...her trusty familiar one thousand and two. You've got a ways to go, but everyone needs to start somewhere.*

# Chapter Thirteen

"I REALLY APPRECIATE this, Kathleen," I responded as I followed her into the kitchen. It was quite beautiful, with modern white cabinets and stainless-steel appliances. The O'Learys had to have someone come into their home on a weekly basis to keep those pots and pans hanging from the ceiling over the island free from dust. There wasn't a smudge of use on them. "I'm not sure what caused this rash."

I'd been able to send a text to Liam of our current predicament before entering the sitting room, so he'd been fully prepared to react when I began to scratch my arm. I didn't keep my nails that long, but I'd created enough of an irritation for my sensitive skin to turn a slight shade of rouge. He feigned concern, asking if Deidre had any antihistamine that I might be able to take. It had worked like a charm, which was surprising given that people usually saw right through me when I was trying to pull a fast one.

*You're baiting me, aren't you? I won't fall for it and give you one of my awesome witty replies. I'm keeping it all to myself. At least, until I get my meds.*

"Allergies can be such a nuisance. I mean, Becca just had a rash on her leg earlier today. I wonder if those storms we've been having recently didn't stir something up in the air."

*Suspect alert! The same woman who talked about hiding evi-*

*dence had a rash on her leg, and probably from the poison she used to kill that poor sheriff. He—*

Leo gasped, and I immediately followed the path his mind had taken from thinking he had a simple allergy to somehow being poisoned with whatever had taken Sheriff O'Leary's life. A quick glance around the kitchen afforded me the ability to see Princess' bowl. Sure enough, the dry food was the kind that had dye added to the mix—the same dye that Leo told me he was allergic to the first time I ever tried to feed him.

*I did? I am? Phew! This short-term memory issue does a number on my heart, sending adrenaline rushing through my overworked body. How is it that I'm not losing weight?*

"It's nice to see that your sister has so much emotional support."

"My sister and I don't always get along, but it's times like these that bring a family closer," Kathleen responded as she continued to rummage through a cupboard that must double as their medicine cabinet. "Here we are. This antihistamine should clear up that rash right away."

*Is that in pill form? That better not be in pill form.*

"Was Deputy Wilson here earlier this morning?" I asked, taking the bottle from Kathleen's hand. I took my time opening it so that I could ask a few questions without Deidre and the other women overhearing our conversation. "I noticed that your sister has his handkerchief. I was just wondering, because Liam and I are heading to the station next. If Deputy Wilson plans on coming back here, then we could save ourselves a trip."

*I know what you're thinking, and it's a plot for one of those daytime dramas that Elsie and Wilma follow every weekday. You're also trying to figure out a way to get me to take that pill that's clearly meant for draft horses. Not happening. My throat isn't going to allow me to take that thing. I'll itch to death first...challenge accepted.*

Of course, it had crossed my mind that Deidre and Deputy Wilson were having an affair. How could it not, especially the way Deidre had been clutching that handkerchief to her chest. One theory could be that Deidre and Deputy Wilson killed Sheriff O'Leary, but then why would Becca be wanting to cover up evidence? What if by evidence, she meant something completely innocent? Then all fingers would still point toward Deidre and Deputy Wilson.

*Seriously? That brunette had a rash on her leg. The poor dead sheriff died from ingesting poison. Remember, one plus one equals two. And don't think I missed the fact that you put a pill into the palm of your hand. Stick that choking hazard back in that bottle right this minute, Raven Lattice Marigold!*

"I'm not sure how Deidre got ahold of Roger's handkerchief," Kathleen said with a frown on her face. "Maybe Becca had an extra one in her purse. Truthfully, I haven't seen Roger since Pat was murdered, but that's not surprising given that the responsibility of the sheriff's office now falls on his shoulders."

*Another motive. Check. Becca and her deputy husband are most likely the guilty parties. We can go home now. Leave the boulder masquerading as a pill while you're at it. I'll just itch for the next twelve or so hours until the allergic reaction fades.*

"It's never easy losing someone we love."

"Claire hasn't been helping in the least," Kathleen shared with a disappointed sigh and a shake of her head. She took the antihistamine bottle from me and set it back inside the cabinet. I palmed the pill that I would have to somehow trick Leo into swallowing, not wanting to take the chance that his allergic reaction wouldn't get worse. "You would think she'd put aside any hard feelings about that speeding ticket, but she's still sitting on the couch and whispering things to Becca like the rest of us don't notice."

*Worse? You're just trying to get me to make this easy for you, but that's not going to happen. No way, no how. I'm not swallowing that horse pill.*

"Speeding ticket?" I inquired, looking on as Kathleen closed the cupboard before walking over to the sink. Her bracelets clinked together in harmony. "Oh? When did Sheriff O'Leary stop Claire for speeding?"

*Huh. Look at that. The antique lady is getting you a glass out of the cabinet. I'm so sorry to have to tell you this, but you're just going to have to take one for the team. She'll know something is up if you don't swallow that rock.*

The antihistamine I held in my hand wasn't a horse pill. As a matter of fact, it wasn't even close. The tiny tablet was no bigger than one of Leo's kitty treats back at the house that I've seen him swallow whole on more than one occasion.

*Size is relative.*

"Rightly so that Pat stopped Claire speeding in that little Mustang of hers, and right in the middle of town. She's going to kill someone if she's not more careful." Kathleen warned, having retrieved the glass and was holding it against a lever that was built into the refrigerator. "No one should get special treatment from the law just because he or she is friends with the sheriff. This happened a couple of months ago, and Deidre's been saying how tense their card nights have become since then. My sister really does need to start choosing her friends more wisely."

A muffled thud came from across the room, no doubt Leo trying to reach that itch on the back of his neck. I quickly continued the discussion with Kathleen to take her mind off the distraction.

"I did notice their heads together and a bit of whispering going on between them," I admitted, making sure there was a bit of reluctance in my tone at sharing such a rude act during such a tragic time. "I take it that Becca agrees with Claire that Sheriff O'Leary shouldn't have conducted the traffic stop?"

*Incoming!*

Leo's warning came a bit too late, and I'd already finished asking my question aloud. I winced at how insensitive I sounded talking out of turn in the kitchen of a grieving widow.

"Go ahead and tell her Kathleen," Deidre said in disdain, though there were tears gathered in her eyes. "Everyone thinks that just because we were born into money that everyday problems don't plague us. I fear we might deal with more in our relationships."

*They aren't dealing with an itch from an allergic reaction that might have me losing my...oh, no! It's back!*

Leo was referring to Princess, whose tail was currently puffed larger than pink cotton candy on a stick. He was going to have to make a run for it, because there was little I could do in the presence of these two sisters. Plus, a break in the case might very well be on the horizon.

"You don't have to—"

I'd been about to protest Deidre's request from her sister to share with me something that was obviously painful, even though it might very well solve this murder mystery. Kathleen stopped me by handing me the glass of water and talking over me.

"There was a rumor circling a few weeks ago that Pat was having an affair with Becca." Kathleen pursed her lips as Deidre dabbed her eyes with Deputy Wilson's handkerchief. Had

Deputy Wilson known about the affair? "Between the speeding ticket and hurtful rumors, the group just hasn't been the same."

"Kathleen, I need to go lie down for a bit," Deidre exclaimed in exhaustion, leaning down and scooping up Princess before the agitated kitty cat could locate Leo and air out his presence. No wonder the poor woman didn't know how to handle her husband's death. "Will you see our guests out?"

This just went to show that appearances were never quite as accurate as one might guess. Deidre had all but shouted the support of her friends from the rooftop upon our arrival, but it had all been done to keep Liam and I from seeing the truth. Having to do so any longer seemed to have been too much for the grieving widow, and she'd gotten to the point where she needed to take care of her own physical well-being.

"Of course," Kathleen responded, true sympathy laced inside those words. Tragedy did have a way of bringing family together. "I'll bring you in a cup of tea shortly. Raven, you take that antihistamine before your rash gets any worse. I'll meet you back in the sitting room."

I mumbled a thank you and an apology all at once, noticing that the palm of my hand hadn't tingled in the slightest since the three of us had begun talking in the kitchen. Did that mean that Deidre and Kathleen had nothing to do with Sheriff O'Leary's murder?

*It could mean the storm has passed, seeing as we've been here for hours already. Your danger meter has been a little wonky lately. Oh, look at that. My itch seems to be better. You can throw that horse pill down the garbage disposal, Raven. No need to take any medication now that the itch is gone. Shall we head back home?*

"You can stop with the delay tactics," I whispered, emptying out the glass of water into the drain. I set what had to be a cut crystal tumbler in the sink, careful not to tip it over. "I can hear you rubbing your back against the corner of the stool. At least let me scratch your back before we join the others."

*Fine, but only a scratch. Don't you dare come near me with that horse pill.*

If I'd had the time, I would have concocted an enchanted blend of catnip for Leo to ingest in order to get rid of his allergic reaction. He definitely wouldn't have complained then, but I didn't have the right components…and generic catnip was definitely out of the equation.

"Come here, big fella," I encouraged, using the center island as a shield from either entrance someone might come through unexpectedly. His whiskers continued to twitch, and I'd swear his left eye was trained on my left hand. I wiggled the fingers of my right in enticement. "I'll scratch your back if you come closer."

*You can't fool me, woman. I'm going to keep my incisors closed tightly together, so no need for your tricks.*

Leo sighed with contentment as I slid my fingers through his fur, scratching until he finally let his guard down a little. I didn't feel bad in the least when his mouth parted, and I used the opportunity to plop the itsy-bitsy pill onto his tongue. Scooping him up in my arms to prevent him from spitting out the capsule was another thing altogether. I'm pretty sure we looked as if we were on some high school wrestling team, with arms and legs entangled every which a way. I happened to come out victorious when I was able to wrestle him on the ground and threaten to change my PayPal password so that he wouldn't be able to order his premium organic catnip from Honduras.

"There," I managed to say as I leaned back against the lower cabinet to catch my breath. I'm pretty sure Leo was close to thirty pounds, and it wasn't as if I worked out on a daily basis. I'd even go so far as to say that our skirmish constituted my exercise for the month. "Give it twenty minutes, and you should get a bit of relief from that itch."

I was saved from hearing a long-winded lecture from Leo when Liam came around the corner. It was a good thing no one else had joined him, because neither Leo or I had the strength to move.

"What on earth did you do to him?" Liam exclaimed in horror as he took in the view before him. A quick glance revealed that Leo looked a bit worse for wear, with his fur tufting in places where it was usually smooth. His head was tilted at an odd angle, and he was rubbing his tongue on the roof of his mouth as if he could somehow spit the pill out onto the floor. It certainly made for an odd sight. "Do we need to take him to see Dr. Jameson?"

"No," I murmured with relief, taking Liam's hand when he offered to help me stand up from the floor. I had Leo's fur all over my shirt and skirt, as well as some of it sticking to my skin. On the bright side, my arms were a bit irritated from the skirmish. The slight redness gave the allergy story a bit more credibility. "I got Leo to swallow the antihistamine, but it sure wasn't easy."

*You're slowly making your way onto my nemesis list, you oath betrayer.*

"I love you," I corrected Leo, setting my hands on my hips to give my declaration a bit more oomph. "And the last thing in the world I can handle is losing you over some red dye in some generic cat food. There are things that you tell me for my own good, and I reciprocate. We're each other's responsibilities, and we must never forget that...even when it means an itsy-bitsy wrestling match every now and then."

Leo seemed to be contemplating my words while going to the extreme and attempting to hack up the pill. Thankfully, nothing come up.

*Raven two…her trusty familiar still one thousand and two. I'm not worried, and I'm going to pretend today didn't happen.*

"Are you two always like this?" Liam asked in what appeared to be a very serious question. He had no idea what Leo was thinking, and I had to remember that he'd only just found out earlier this afternoon about my abilities, along with the fact that Leo was my familiar. "Don't answer that. Listen, we need to drive back to Paramour Bay. I have some questions for Lydia. Jack is meeting us there, too."

I blew Leo a kiss, which I'm pretty sure had him rolling that left eye of his before we began making our way back to the sitting room. There were many things we needed to talk about on our trip back to Paramour Bay, such as the fact that the residents of this town suspected Sheriff O'Leary was having an affair with Becca Wilson. And when the time came, I still needed to share with Liam that Ted was a wax golem. I hadn't wanted to reveal too much, too soon.

*Karma.*

Leo was going to one-line me all the way home, but the fact that he wouldn't go into some type of true asthma attack made it all worth it. I, on the other hand, might need some sort of inhaler while waiting for Liam's reaction on the whole wax golem thing.

*You wouldn't be saying it was worth it if I had choked on that horse pill. And just so you know, you also still have to explain how the broomstick was stolen right out of the good ol' sheriff's office inside a locked police station. I'll have a front row seat on the middle console with the cool air from the vent blowing right in my face the whole time.*

Well, maybe Leo wasn't going to be one-lining it all the way home. I had a feeling the drive was going to be very, very long.

# Chapter Fourteen

*I* *HATE FEELING bad over something. It's like when I'm chasing Skippy through the neighborhood and he inadvertently lands in Newt's yard with that big old English bulldog just waiting to join in on the chase. It's a wonder Skippy hasn't lost a limb or two from those accidental close encounters.*

Leo wasn't the only one feeling bad over the fact that Liam was still trying to absorb the fact that my mother had actually broken into the police station and stolen evidence from an active investigation. His knuckles had no color in them now that he was gripping the steering wheel hard enough that it was a wonder it hadn't snapped in two.

*Speaking of snapped, it's a good thing you left out the Ted bombshell until later. That might have been enough to shatter the good ol' sheriff's sanity into a billion pieces. He'd be foaming at the mouth by now, and we'd all die when he ran off the road. I can't believe this. I've got a front row seat to seeing your mother hauled off to jail, and it's completely free of charge.*

"How am I going to explain that I've lost a major piece of evidence in a homicide investigation to Jack?" Liam asked, an underlying hint of anger breaking through his tentative composure. I don't think I've ever heard him get mad before. "I signed the broomstick out of the state evidence locker, Raven. I'm responsible for it. Me. You need to call your mother and have her put the broomstick back on my desk before we arrive at the station."

*Your mother sure knows how to throw those monkey wrenches around, doesn't she? Someone was bound to get hit in the head sooner or later.*

The thing of it was…I actually understood Liam's total frustration. He could lose his job over my mother's thoughtless choices. Something like this could ruin his reputation in the law enforcement community, and it wasn't like anyone would believe him should he start spouting nonsense about witches and hexes.

*Again, now you're just making me feel bad. I can't take it anymore. Just call your mother and have her fix this horrible situation. After all, this is her mess to clean up anyway.*

I let the deafening silence fill the cab as I retrieved my phone from my skirt pocket. Purses weren't my thing, so I kept my license and credit card in a small pocket attached to my cell phone case. I constructed a quick text, mindful of saying too much. There was just enough instruction for my mother to understand the severity of why she needed to fix this problematic situation.

The only way my predicament could go further south was if Mom had decided to return to the city. I wouldn't put something like that past her, especially when I'd told her to stay clear of the antique shop. Granted, she'd probably love spending time playing house at the tea shop with Beetle, but she wouldn't want to stay too long for fear of running into me.

*I've been thinking about the time Regina worked on that home-school project your grandmother had assigned to her all those years ago. The details are still fuzzy, but Rowena was so darn adamant she'd never heard of such a hexed item associated with the Barnes family. Trust me, nothing gets past that woman.*

I would have asked Leo more questions on that topic, but Liam was already too much on edge. He'd taken the entire story about witchcraft, casting spells, and invisible familiars in stride, but my mother's side adventure of breaking into the police station to steal evidence had proven a bit too much for one day's adventures.

"Liam, I would never let my family's history of witchcraft ruin your life. Never in a million years."

He remained silent, checking his rearview mirror a time or two, but I'm pretty sure that was just to give him something to do so that he didn't have to talk to me right now. The intake of information today had been overwhelming even for him. For the most part, he'd taken everything in stride. Now all I needed was for him to believe that I would never allow a fouled-up magic broomstick to take away his career as sheriff.

*You know that I'm not for all that sappy stuff, but you should be very cautious on what guarantees you offer in this situation, my dear Raven. You only have control over your own abilities. Your mother is an entirely different animal.*

Leo's usual theatrics had been put aside as he hammered home another lesson. As much as he might have his annual squirrel battles, his conspiracy theories, and his raging addiction to exotic Honduran catnip, he really did have my best interest at heart.

"There are many rules of the coven," I began, keeping my cell phone in my hand so that I could read my mother's answer as soon as she responded. "Even though I'm not a part of the coven, the guidelines are there for all of our protection. First and foremost, no witch or wizard should use magic for their own gain. There are supernatural repercussions for doing so, and those consequences can be pretty severe."

*Really? Now who is hammering home a nail in the proverbial coffin lid?*

I reached over and stroked Leo's back, letting him know that I hadn't been talking about his looks. That necromancy spell had done a number on him, but he'd made the sacrifice to stay behind for me. I would be eternally grateful for such a selfless act.

*There you go again, getting all mushy-gushy on me.*

"Magic is to be used for the all-encompassing good," I continued, needing Liam to understand that I would never let him be hurt by my family. Leo was right in that I couldn't control everything, but I could protect him from my mother's bad choices. "Witchcraft should be utilized to help others, which I would do in a heartbeat to protect you. My mom might have had ulterior motives for stealing the broomstick from the security of the police station, but your life was in danger. She thought she was protecting you. No one knows how long the broomstick needs to be in one's possession before the curse takes hold. I'll make sure that my mother has the original item returned—minus the hex—or that an exact replica is produced and put into its place so that no one else is the wiser."

Right on cue, my cell phone vibrated and displayed my mother's response. Let's just say that she was a bit offended that I would believe she hadn't thought to cover her tracks, and that she would never expose our family's abilities to the sheriff of Paramour Bay, of all people.

*Oh, I can't wait to see the expression on your mother's face when you tell her that you already spilled the witchcraft beans. My BFF better have brought me another satchel of premium organic catnip so that I have something to munch on during the fireworks display later tonight.*

"Mom took care of it," I shared with such a huge sense of relief that I had to lean my head back against the headrest. "No one will ever know that the broomstick in your possession isn't the original one, which is currently buried to protect others against the curse."

*Maybe it's because I'm in a good mood now that my itching has subsided—not that I don't think it wouldn't have gone away on its own—but I'm proposing another trip to see Rowena. I'm beginning to feel we're getting the old runaround from your mother. If we need to lower our standards to use Rowena against her, then so be it. And no, this isn't the horse pill talking. Or is it? Does antihistamine boost courage? Asking for a friend.*

A little bit of color began to gradually return to Liam's hands, but it was evident that he was still struggling with everything that I've laid on his doorstep today.

*You mean the bombshell of all witchy bombshells?*

"This is going to take some getting used to, isn't it?" Liam said, finally getting ready to flip his turn signal so we could take the exit to the long and winding road that would take us back to Paramour Bay. "I'm not quite sure how I feel about evidence in a major felony investigation being replaced by a replica. With that said and if this curse does exist, I wouldn't want to be responsible for someone else falling victim to some horrible death curse."

"It's a lot to shoulder," I replied softly, glad when Liam reached in front of Leo to hold my hand. I ignored Leo's imitation of hacking up a hairball. "The learning curve is pretty steep, and I can admit to not being a fast learner."

*You're understating the obvious. The good ol' sheriff really ought to know what he's getting himself into, you know. If you can make my tail go numb for hours, I can only imagine the risk Liam would be taking with his—*

"Is Leo trying to tell me something?" Liam asked, cutting off Leo's incessant meowing. "He seems very adamant right now."

*Hand, Raven. You know, the one he needs to do his job? If my life is in danger, I'd like for him to be able to reach for his firearm. Get your mind out of the gutter and listen.*

"Leo gets a bit frustrated with me on my learning curve," I replied wryly, ready to switch topics. "Liam, I learned some things while I was in the kitchen with Kathleen and Deidre that put an entirely new spin on the direction of your case."

"You mean the fact that Deidre believes that her husband was having an affair with Becca Wilson?" Liam had already driven down the off ramp and was making sure the coast was clear before pulling onto the two-lane road. "Laura Midleaf pulled me aside while you were getting Leo some antihistamine. The other two women weren't happy that she requested to speak with me in private, but Mrs. Midleaf is tired of all the lies and deception within their small group. They've been friends for many years, but it's not been without their fair share of small-town drama."

"Doesn't that give Deidre motive? I feel bad for even suggesting that she could be responsible, but I also know the spouse is usually the prime suspect in these types of cases."

I fully expected Leo to give his two cents, but he remained quiet. The two vents in the dashboard were still blowing cool air in his direction, and he was enjoying the slight breeze with his eyes closed. On the bright side, he wasn't continually scratching anymore. The antihistamine had kicked in a few miles back.

"This is what we know so far," Liam began to share as he made himself a bit more comfortable in the driver's seat now that he didn't have to worry about explaining missing evidence.

"Deputy Wilson went hiking last weekend, stumbled over something sticking out of the ground, and dug up the broom. He brought it back to the station with him, where it stayed until Sheriff O'Leary said he'd drive it to the antique shop to see if Kathleen or Lydia might think it was worth money and want to sell it from their shop."

"Sell it?" This was the first I was hearing about such an exchange. "Why would Sheriff O'Leary believe a broom was worth anything, and who told you this?"

"Becca did after you left the room to take your phone call." Liam lifted his left hand to wave at a passing vehicle. "Anyway, Sheriff O'Leary thought the branded *B* on the handle meant it was some sort of recognizable antique. One with a history."

A soft snore began to carry throughout the cab of the truck. That antihistamine must have really done a number on Leo.

"And that's it?" I asked, having truly believed there was something more to the story. "What about the list of herbs that Sheriff O'Leary had clutched in his hand when he died?"

"Let's back up to the morning he left the station. Becca was there, and we now have two different versions of what happened before Sheriff O'Leary left for Paramour Bay. Deputy Wilson claims that there was no mention of Paramour Bay, which his wife contradicts. Their account of that day doesn't match, but neither Jack nor I are ready to point that out without first talking with Lydia."

"One of them is obviously lying. Do you think that Deputy Wilson found out about the affair between his boss and wife? Does Jack believe that Deputy Wilson killed Sheriff O'Leary?"

"Possibly, but we can't rule out Deidre O'Leary," Liam pointed out. "She cooked her husband breakfast that morning. What's not to say she didn't mix in some of those herbs on his list?"

"I never did see the list of herbs that Sheriff O'Leary had in his possession," I reminded Liam, not that I would be able to tell what Sheriff O'Leary had ingested or who might have given it to him. I imagine that Jack would be getting the autopsy report any day now. "I find it hard to believe that he didn't mention a thing to anyone about poisonous herbs, plants, or roots, especially if he suspected that he might be poisoned by his wife soon."

"Here." Liam had set his cell phone in the cup holder of the console Leo was currently sacked out on. "Pull up my text messages. Jack sent me a picture of the list. The medical examiner knows what kind of poison we're looking for in the bloodwork, but maybe something will stick out for you."

Truthfully, I was surprised that Liam hadn't made the connection between my abilities and the capability of solving the case. I hadn't been able to cast a spell on the broomstick to seek answers, but a piece of paper was another thing altogether. I'd take a look at it first. Afterward, I would see if Liam could get his hands on the list itself for me to perform a quick incantation.

We were now entering Paramour Bay, where the wax museum was located to the left and the iconic Paramour Bay Inn was to my right. I quickly found Jack's name and pressed his text message. I had to scroll down a bit until I came across a photograph of the list that had been in Sheriff O'Leary's hand.

It took all my strength to keep the phone in my hand as shockwaves rushed over me at the alarming discovery before me. This couldn't be happening, and I quickly lowered the phone so that I could look out the windshield.

"Raven?" Liam's concern was apparent, but I didn't have enough air in my lungs to reply. "Raven, what is it?"

*I'm up, I'm up. Why is my fur standing on end? The cab of this truck is like a blanket of static electricity. Whatever you're doing, Raven, stop it this very instant. That was the best sleep I've had in years. Couldn't you have just left me in the truck with the air conditioning running? I don't want to move from this spot.*

"We have a problem," I whispered in horror, lifting the phone one more time to see if anything had changed with the picture in the last four seconds. "A big problem."

*No, we don't. Whatever you are looking at on that phone, turn it off. Problem solved. I'm going back to sleep.*

Liam finally pulled the truck to a stop in front of the police station, shifting the gear into park before taking the phone out of my hand. He studied the picture, but he wouldn't see what I had upon setting eyes on such blasphemy.

*Blasphemy? Photograph?*

"I don't see what the problem is," Liam finally confessed, his curious and concerned gaze lifting from the display to settle on what I was sure was complete devastation written across my face. "Talk to me, Raven."

"I know that handwriting."

*Handwriting? Broomstick? Ohhhh, this isn't good, Raven. My memory is returning, and I really don't like the images I'm getting from way back then. I never thought I'd say this, but I might be in need of another horse pill. You won't have to trick me this time…promise.*

"You know who wrote this list?" Liam asked, holding up the phone when I truly had no desire to look at it anymore.

*No, you don't. You think you do, but you really don't. My memory could be playing tricks on me. It's possible. Can there be side effects if one combines generic horrible tasting catnip with an antihistamine? That's it! This is all a bad dream! Well, technically a nightmare, and it's all due to that massive horse pill. Tell me I'm right, Raven.*

"The handwriting on that list belongs to my mother," I managed to say as a hot flash washed over me. I quickly turned one of Leo's vents my way, leaning forward so the cool air would hit my face. "This is bad. This is really bad."

*I don't care about side effects anymore. Give me another horse pill, Raven! Knock me out. Go ahead, because you Marigold women are going to be the death of me yet.*

That's what I was afraid of…that my mother was somehow responsible for the death of Sheriff O'Leary.

*Ten minutes. I slept more peacefully in ten minutes than I have in years, and you had to go and wake me up to a witchcraft apocalypse started by your mother. I always knew she'd be the death of me.*

# *Chapter Fifteen*

"BEETLE, THANK YOU so much for reopening the store," I exclaimed with a stiff smile plastered across my face. It was actually a little after five o'clock, so I hadn't been so sure I'd catch him or my mother in the shop. I was more concerned that my mother might have actually headed back into the city, figuring it was only a matter of time before I realized where that list of poisonous components had come from. "I really appreciate it."

*Don't you dare let my BFF walk out that door without giving me a bit of that premium organic catnip that he has stored in the front pocket of his dress shirt. I can smell it from here. I need all the help I can get to make it through this upcoming confrontation with your mother.*

"My pleasure, Raven," Beetle replied, adjusting his bowtie. "My pleasure. We didn't have much foot traffic after the power finally came back on, but Bree did stop in for that inventory you set aside for the bakery. Your mother just went into the back to put the check in the safe. I thought that best given the amount."

I attempted to cover up my tremendous relief that I would be able to have this upcoming skirmish with my mother in person. She always had a tendency to hang up the phone way too soon when I was attempting to extract information from her. We needed to have this conversation face to face.

*You're assuming that your mother is still in the backroom and hasn't slipped out the exit upon our return. You give that woman too much credit, Raven.*

I would know better what I was dealing with if Leo would just come clean about what he recalled from the time my mother buried the so-called hexed broomstick. At this point, I wasn't even sure that was the case.

*Me, either. My brain is mush, and I blame that horse pill you forced on me. Although, my sinuses sure are clear.*

My mother wasn't the only one who knew how to use a stall tactic.

*I have no idea what you're talking about, Raven.*

"How is my boy doing in this heat?" Beetle asked, walking over to where Leo had already collapsed on his pillow in the display window. Sure enough, a bit of catnip was being sprinkled in the corner as if this were any other day. "There you go, my friend. There you go."

*I love him so much. I wish I could warn him off your mother.*

"You know what?" I needed to distract Beetle long enough have a private conversation with my mother. "You and Mom deserve a nice dinner on me, so why don't you head on over to the diner to grab a table. You know how busy that place can be around this time of day. I'll send her over after I have a little chat with her about Aunt Rowena. Her birthday is coming up, and I thought we'd go in on a gift for her together."

*For someone who is such a horrible liar, that was one smooth con.*

Desperation. That was my only excuse, because normally I would have broken out into hives by now. Truthfully, I had no clue when Aunt Rowena celebrated her birthday.

"What a wonderful idea, Raven! Wonderful idea," Beetle

said after patting Leo on the head and leaving my familiar to indulge in his favorite pastime. "Let your mother know I'll try to grab our favorite booth. It was where I first looked into those green eyes of hers and realized that she was the one for me."

*Why do all of you people have the knack for making me want to hack up a hairball?*

"Mother, come out here right this second," I demanded after the bell chimed above the entrance to signify that Beetle had exited the shop. "Now!"

*If I didn't know what was about to be discussed, I would have enjoyed this front view seat with my delicious snack.*

"Maybe we could have avoided this confrontation if you had told me what I wanted to know about the curse," I muttered, still not hearing the ivory-colored fairy beads conduct their melodic clicks to indicate my mother was coming out of her hiding place. "Mom, I'm serious. I want the truth. A man's life was taken by poison, and the list he had clutched inside his hand at the time of his death was written by you."

*Yep. That caught the Queen Witch's attention.*

"I had nothing to do with that man's death, Raven Lattice," my mother defiantly exclaimed, appearing through the ivory-colored fairies as if nothing was wrong. She walked quickly to the counter and placed both hands on the hard surface anxiously as she leaned toward me. "The incantation that I utilized on the dirt where the broomstick was buried showed exactly who dug it up. How was it even possible for that deputy to know there was something underneath all that undergrowth?"

"Deputy Wilson simply tripped over it," I divulged, noting that Mom still hadn't addressed the list of material components. "I guess the rain washed away some of the dirt over the years and a bit of the handle was eventually exposed. Where did Sheriff

O'Leary obtain that list, Mom?"

*My memory returned, Regina. You might as well tell your daughter everything, because she's really good at force feeding one a horse pill. There's no telling what she can do to make you talk.*

"One thing a mother never wants is to disappoint her own daughter."

I shot Leo a glare, a part of me realizing that this moment was very hard for my mother. The vulnerability across her aging yet beautiful features was quite evident, but I needed to hear the truth regarding the cursed broomstick.

"Mom, no one is perfect. That includes you," I replied softly, reaching for her hands. I clasped her fingers, causing her green gaze to meet mine. Once again, I was astounded by the helplessness I saw there. "Tell me. It can't be worse than some of the things I've done in my attempt to learn what little witchcraft I command thus far."

*I hate to be the bearer of bad news, but I'm pretty sure causing a man to be dead is worse than prompting my tail to turn numb. Just thought I'd point that one out.*

"Thank you, Leo," my mother said wryly with a roll of her eyes. She inhaled deeply, as if to find the strength she'd need to carry through with the conversation. She squeezed my fingers in what I assumed was supposed to be reassurance, but we were talking about murder…whether intentional or not. "Raven, you know that I love you."

*Diversion tactic number one. Don't fall for it, Raven.*

"I might not have been the perfect mother, but I did try my best to shield you from the same mistakes I made when I was younger."

My mother and I both arched our brows toward Leo as a warning not to comment or add in his two cents. His head whipped up from the catnip he was munching on, a few of the green particles stuck to his upper lip in between his whiskers.

"I was telling the truth about that research project your grandmother wanted me to write when I was fourteen as part of my witchcraft learning." Mom released my hands and stood before beginning to walk around the tea shop to rid herself of the apprehensive energy I could sense in the room. She no longer looked at me directly as she recalled the past. "I made it a point to always strive for bigger and better, and I didn't want to research some well-known artifact that we'd heard about a thousand times over. So, I went looking for something unique, which meant speaking with those in the coven. Long story short, one of the Barnes' ancestors had passed away from a heart attack. Soon after that, the same son who had inherited her belongings had fallen off a ladder to his death. Rumors began to circulate, and somehow the broomstick was mentioned in passing due to it belonging to Lucille Rebecca Barnes at the time of her death. One thing led to another, and I had somehow convinced myself that the broomstick had been hexed and was the perfect subject for my project."

I remained silent, not wanting to interrupt my mother while she was finally sharing a piece of her childhood with me. It was most likely foolish, but I was still holding out hope that this had all been a big mistake.

"How amazing would it be if I could devise a spell to reverse the hex?"

My mother's question was hypothetical, of course, but I could see where this was going a mile away.

*I wish I was a mile away. Oops. That slipped out. Carry on.*

"I wrote a list of material components that I'd need, stole the object in question from a house up in Windsor, and proceeded to search for the rare material components I needed for close to a month. It wasn't easy, but I managed to get everything I thought I'd need for the counter-enchantment. I was also keeping detailed notes so that I could show your grandmother how I not only successfully found a cursed item, but that I'd actually reversed the hex."

"Leo, where were you during this time?" I asked in disbelief, completely flabbergasted that a fourteen-year-old girl could have gotten away with something so dangerous. Technically, Mom hadn't come away unscathed, but I still couldn't fathom how Nan and Leo had allowed something like this to unfold. "Or Nan?"

"Oh, Leo isn't to blame for my wayward ways back in the day," my mother said with a soft laugh and what sounded a lot like endearment. "His role was to aid and advise your grandmother. Not me. I could have easily called forth my own familiar if I'd wanted one, but I'd had no desire to deal with any of that at the time. You have to understand, it was different then. In the summer, we were sent out to play as long as we were back for dinner or when the sun set. Plus, I had the ability to defend myself. I wasn't nearly as awkward as you were at that age, darling."

*I'm not so sure that I should have mixed catnip with that horse pill, Raven. I must be hallucinating, because I'm pretty sure I heard a compliment come out of your mother's mouth. Not one for you, though. Sorry, not sorry.*

"Long story short, it turned out that the broomstick wasn't cursed at all, but I had somehow attached a hex to it myself. An utter and complete failure." My mom was now standing near the display window, watching vehicles drive by now and then. She had her arms crossed and those red lips of hers curled up in what appeared to be a somewhat sad smile. "I realized what was happening halfway through the incantation, but I wasn't sure what would happen if I stopped midway through. Of course, I ran straight to your grandmother once I grasped the severity of the situation. She handled it well, explaining that testing one's boundaries was a good thing as long as we had fail-safes in place. She simply tucked the piece of paper I'd written the components on inside the birch twigs, drove me out to the woods around thirty miles from here, and she told me to bury it handle up where it could never be found."

"Why wouldn't Nan have tried to erase the hex you some-how crafted by mistake?" I asked, at a loss as to why this situation had to be made so complicated back then. "It wasn't technically a true curse, was it?"

*I'm still thinking about that compliment. Did you hear it, Raven? Or was I hallucinating? Maybe I'm still asleep in the truck. Hey, tell the good ol' sheriff to hit a pothole so I can stop dreaming. Maybe that will be enough to wake me up and this will have been nothing but a nightmare.*

"Think of witchcraft like baking." My mother finally turned to face me, leaving Leo to ponder about the side effects of his catnip and antihistamine. "One can throw in a lot of ingredients and pull out either a delicious creation or something atrocious from the oven. Apply that to witchcraft. What does a cook do when something they create can't be eaten? Throw it away, of course. Your grandmother understood that the best course of action in response to my mistake was to bury the item in question."

*Rosemary was such a wise witch. I do miss her so.*

"Let me understand this correctly," I said, wanting to pause the discussion for just a moment while I verified the timeline.

"You basically sought out an object that wasn't exactly cursed—thinking it was—and then caused it to be semi-hexed by casting a spell on said item. What do you think the ramifications would be to anyone in possession of the broomstick?"

"I don't know, and that was the problem," my mother confessed with a sigh of resignation. "My darling Raven, that was the first time I realized what kind of power I held in my hands. Knowing that I could be responsible for someone's death with a few material components and some words was overwhelming, and it took your grandmother months to convince me to resume my home studies."

*Teenagers…so dramatic.*

Both my mother and I once again turned toward Leo in exasperation.

*Oh, did I think that aloud? That's turning into a very bad habit.*

I'd never fully understood how my mother could walk away from something so important as our history. The amount of good that we were able to do in this world was insurmountable, and I now somehow felt responsible to the residents of Paramour Bay to help them in any way I could. Would I have felt the same at the age of fourteen? Realizing the consequences of such mistakes might have been enough for me to turn my back on witchcraft forever, just like my mother.

*This is your destiny, Raven.*

"And you went through overwhelming odds to be here, and I'll be forever be grateful," I responded genuinely. "Do you remember when I thought my love enchantment had somehow begun setting fires around town? Do you recall how worried I was that my actions had caused that kind of damage? I'm an adult and had a hard time accepting such responsibility. I can only imagine what was going through Mom's young mind at the time."

"Young mind at the time?" my mother reiterated with that arched brow of hers. "Age is just a number, my dear. I'm still quite young at heart."

*Don't you dare start talking about my BFF, or I'll have to hack up this delicious catnip that I've just finished. Images like that sear my brain, and I don't have many more brain cells left to lose wastefully.*

"If the broomstick was never properly cursed and you buried it with whatever spell you managed to attach to it at the time, then how did it end up on some website about hexed items?" I asked, not wanting to leave any loose ends when I walked down to the antique store to join Liam. He was going to be very happy to hear that the broomstick wasn't the cause of any deaths. "Ted also told me the broomstick had a dreadful curse attached to it."

*It does have a spell attached to it. Ted must have thought you were talking about the one your mother cast upon it, because I now recall discussing with him all about your mother's glory years. What can I say? I must have been having a senior moment.*

"Glory years?" Mom practically snorted her disbelief before shaking her head in sadness. "Raven, you need to understand that was my very first time I truly comprehended the responsibility of our family's practice. By the time I was pregnant with you, I couldn't continue with that life. I wanted the normality of an eight to five job, raising my daughter, and not having to worry that I could hurt someone if I made a mistake."

"You say that, but you *did* continue to utilize magic," I pointed out, having looked back at the odd times something had worked out for me that had been against the odds. "I hadn't known it then, but I do now."

"Oh, a sprinkle of magic here and there is nothing like what you've been doing these past ten months," my mother said with a wave of her hand. She seemed rather sincere in the pride that laced her tone. "Honey, why do you think I've been so vigilant in watching over you? I don't want you doing something where the guilt is insurmountable. I don't believe I've ever told you this, but you are so much like your grandmother—vibrant, determined, and practically unstoppable when it comes to your incessant need to help others. Your sense of self-preservation is almost nonexistent, whereas mine has always been in the forefront. I'm not a bad person, Raven. I just know my limitations. The day I had you was the exact moment my heart was given arms and legs, and I realized that my powers were given to me in order to protect you as best I could."

My mother had never been the helicopter-type mom who hovered over every single detail of my life, nor had she ever been one of the touchy-feely variety. To know what she'd experienced on the day of my birth stole any reprimand that might have been on the tip of my tongue for the way she'd handled leaving town at the age of twenty-four, raising me unaware of our lineage, and meddling in the new life that I'd been handed by my grandmother after she passed.

I also recognized that it hadn't been easy for my mother to confess her mistakes and reveal the vulnerabilities she'd faced in the aftermath. There was no doubt that she would do something within five minutes that had me clenching my fists and gritting my teeth, but I wasn't going to pass up this heart-warming moment.

"Oh, Mom," I said, walking around the counter so that I could hold her tight. "I wish you would have told me this years ago or even ten months ago. It would have made a world of difference."

*What is happening? Why are you two…hugging? Sweet angel of mercy, did the squirrel apocalypse finally happen while I was napping? It's just like I've been predicting all these years!*

As I'd mentioned, my mother wasn't fond of public displays of affection. She laughed awkwardly and patted my back, giving me what I needed in the moment. Leo's short-term memory would no doubt return any second. Now that we'd solved the broomstick mystery, it was time to crack Sheriff O'Leary's murder case.

*You just had to remind me, didn't you? One day of normalcy isn't too much to ask for, is it? That reminds me, I do need to take a mental health day soon.*

"Well, now that you know just how burdensome the responsibility of witchcraft can be…is there any chance I can convince you to finally come back to the city?" my mother asked, having already pulled away and was picking off a mysteriously absent piece of lint from her white blouse.

That moment where I'd be clenching my fists and gritting my teeth came faster than I'd expected, but I counted to ten so as not to spoil our moment, however brief.

*Try twenty. I've found that ten doesn't quite do it for me.*

"Not a chance, Mom. Besides, Beetle is waiting for you over at the diner," I reminded her as I ushered her toward the door. "I'm meeting Liam at the antique shop to speak with Lydia. Now that we know the broomstick wasn't involved, we can tailor our questions to be more specific."

*Or we can let the good ol' sheriff do his own job for once. I vote we drive back to the cottage, be thankful for air conditioning, and recover from these last couple of horrible days by vegging on the couch and watching old reruns of "Bewitched" on Hulu.*

"I'm in agreement with Leo," my mother advised, causing Leo to choke on some of the catnip morsels he was trying not to waste. It was rare my mother and Leo agreed on anything. "Let Liam handle his investigation. Come join Beetle and me for a bite to eat. Leo can veg all on his own."

Mom had no idea that I'd spilled the witchcraft beans to Liam, and that's how it was going to stay. We'd already exited the tea shop, but I'd made sure to switch over the closed sign and lock up to secure the store. Now, I needed to hurry up and see to it that my mother quickly made her way to the diner. The last thing I needed was for Leo to materialize and blurt out the fact that I'd told Liam we were witches. If that should happen, my mother might actually try to hire someone to kidnap me and take me back to the city.

"I already promised Liam that I'd join him for dinner, Mom." I pasted a smile on my face, but this time I couldn't pull off the lie. She saw right through me. This was the best time to cut and run. "Gotta go. Love you! Text me if you're staying in town overnight. I'll make sure the couch is made up for you."

"Oh, darling," my mother said rather coyly. I held up a hand to stop her from sharing too much, which she had an overabundant need to do at times like this, but it was too late. "If I'm going to stay in town, I certainly won't be using your couch. I'll touch base with you in the morning. In the meantime, try to stay out of trouble. Ta-ta!"

*My ears are burning! My ears are burning!*

"We knew it was going to happen eventually," I muttered, observing my mother walk across the street as if she owned the town. She was certainly a force to be reckoned with, which was why it was still hard to comprehend the vulnerability she'd displayed just a few moments ago. "You don't think…"

*That your mother just played you like a world class violinist?*

*Considering those horrid memories that she dredged up for me, that research project of hers was definitely the beginning of the end of her fascination with magic and the birth of her desire to leave town. On the other hand, I wouldn't put it past Regina to somehow plant false recollections in my head. Once again, I find myself in need of a recuperation day. This job should really come with hazard pay.*

"It does," I said with a laugh. We continued to walk on the sidewalk, passing the malt shop and Mindy's boutique. I was always careful talking to Leo in public. Technically, he could read my thoughts, but you'd be surprised at how difficult it was to carry on a conversation in that manner. "Catnip. Very expensive catnip that somehow keeps showing up on our front doorstep."

Speaking of doorsteps, we'd finally arrived at the entrance of the antique shop. Liam was inside, probably already having questioned Lydia about the broomstick and the list of herbal components. My arrival would signal that death by a hexed broomstick was definitely out of the equation.

*I wouldn't say that. Did you notice that your mother evaded the question about where she buried said hexed broomstick? So help me if she buried it underneath my window at the cottage. I wouldn't put it past her, you know. I'd have to make it my mission to haunt her until the end of all time.*

"We have enough problems than to add on worrying about a broomstick that we don't even know what it could do, given the right circumstances," I reminded Leo, wrapping my fingers around the handle of the glass door in front of me. "Let's help Liam, and then we can finally talk about that mental health day."

*Speaking of recovery, that horse pill might have been the best sleeping anecdote ever created. Is there a liquid form? I'm once again asking for a friend.*

# Chapter Sixteen

"...ANYONE ELSE IN the shop when Sheriff O'Leary stopped in?" Liam was still questioning Lydia as I came to stand next to him in front of the white oak bar height table that served as the shop's payment counter. It was the only piece of furniture in the shop that appeared to be from the current century. I absolutely adored the charming twist instead of the usual laminate counters used in most of the shops in town. "Was there a chance he could have spoken to someone on the way out? Maybe as someone was passing by?"

Jack had already questioned Lydia, so we were already aware that there had been no customers at the time of Sheriff O'Leary's visit. Kathleen had been at an estate auction, and she didn't employ anyone other than Lydia. Why, then, had the palm of my hand begun to tingle?

*Uh, Raven?*

Leo's distant voice told me that he wasn't close by, but instead probably on the other side of the shop. I don't believe that he was talking about the sensation of piercing needles in my palm, but he was still under the effects of the antihistamine. For all I knew, he thought he was standing right next to me and had just wandered underneath the table.

*We have a serious issue, and you want to pretend that I'm still loopy from that horse pill you gave me? Seriously, you need to see these genuine witchcraft items. And I do mean genuine.*

"I don't believe Sheriff O'Leary spoke to anyone on his way out of the shop," Lydia said, twirling a ring on her right hand in a rather uneasy manner. She definitely knew more than she was saying. Had Jack caught on to that fact when he'd taken her statement yesterday? Had something happened in between the time Jack had spoken to her and now? What had she remembered that could help solve this murder? "He came inside and asked me about the broomstick. I gave him what information I could find, and then he left."

*Raven, I really think you need to come over here. The problem I mentioned? It just became bigger than anticipated.*

The bell above the door chimed, causing all three of us to see who had come into the shop. Surprisingly, it was Kathleen. She seemed a bit out of breath, and I'm pretty sure she lost a bit of color at the sight of us. The audible sigh of relief coming from Lydia was unmistakable.

*Speaking of bells…*

"Hello," Kathleen said with a tight smile, breezing past us to join Lydia on the other side of the table. She set down her purse that I was pretty sure was from the 1920s before telling Lydia that she could start closing up the shop. "Is everything okay? Did you find out something new after leaving Deidre's house? I left her at home sleeping, although Becca and Claire are staying while I take care of things here. Laura drove to the funeral home to pick up some pamphlets for my sister to look at when she feels up to it later this evening. I couldn't bring myself to do that, and I used the store as an excuse to leave for a while."

A few things struck me as odd, especially given that Deidre had all but asked Kathleen to see her guests out of the house. I would have, as well, if I'd thought my dead husband had been having an affair with one of my best friends. Also, why would Kathleen leave her sister to take a drive into Paramour Bay when Lydia was more than capable of taking care of things at the shop?

*Can we get back to the bell? This is serious business, Raven.*

"We'll try not to keep you," Liam responded, not too happy that Kathleen had dismissed her assistant. I was being pulled in two different directions, needing to focus on why my palm was warning me of something disastrous to come, as well as Leo's new obsession with bells. "Lydia mentioned the estate sale you attended yesterday. Where did you say that auction took place?"

"Branford," Kathleen replied, reaching for a stack of mail that had been set aside next to the cash register. I noticed that Lydia was practically twirling the ring off of her finger, and she attempted to turn toward the back room. "I drove straight to Deidre's house after hearing what happened to Pat. It wasn't until late last night that I was able to speak with Detective Swanson."

"Lydia, what website did you use to search for information on the broomstick?" I asked, wanting to help Liam out by keeping everyone in one area. It also wouldn't hurt to retain that bit of information for a later date. Myths and legends usually started out from a source. In this case, my mother, but it would be interesting to see if there was anything else listed that I might need to know about down the line. "Maybe somewhere on that site it can explain the list of material components Sheriff O'Leary had with him when he visited that day."

Lydia rattled off a website that I'd never heard of, but I could literally sense the tension coming off of Liam's body as he stood next to me in front of the table. What had I missed? Silence began to fill the shop, and not the comfortable kind. I'd been studying the various incantations in the family grimoire, but none of the spells sprang to mind in order to figure out when this visit had taken a turn for the worse.

*No spells are springing forth, but the bells might be ringing soon. Let me put it to you this way, Raven—you need to solve the case quickly so we can focus on more important things in this shop of horrors.*

Leo definitely had a clear mind. Whatever he'd discovered on the other side of the shop had to be a doozy, but at least he'd tipped me off in that whatever it was he was seeing had nothing to do with Sheriff O'Leary's murder. That left me little choice but to try and figure out why the tension around us was thick enough to cut with a knife.

*Oh, trust me. A knife is the least of our worries.*

Kathleen set the unopened stack of mail back in a spot next to the cash register. She was acting no differently than she had at Deidre's house, yet there had been an energy shift ever since she'd found us speaking with her assistant. It was clear that Kathleen was giving subtle hints that it was time to close up so she could finish what she'd come to do in order to get back to her sister.

Leo's odd quips coming from the other side of the shop were giving me heart palpitations. What could be more important than solving a murder mystery?

*One where we might be the next victims.*

"Branford?" Liam asked, repeating the town's name where Kathleen had stated she'd been when Sheriff O'Leary had visited the shop. I was torn on whether or not to stay by Liam's side or rush to see what Leo had found amongst the inventory that could be so dangerous. "Lydia, didn't you tell Detective Swanson that Kathleen was in Stony Creek?"

The palm of my hand began to harness energy, warning me

that Liam's prodding question had just opened up the floodgates on two possible suspects. Neither Kathleen nor Lydia had motive that I was aware of, but Liam had just caught them skirting the truth.

Just where had Kathleen been the day of Sheriff O'Leary's murder?

*I have no idea, but I know what might have been in this shop. Can you interrupt your conversation and ask either of these horrible fibbers if they've heard any bells ringing lately?*

Kathleen had been reaching for her purse, but her hand stopped midway upon hearing Liam's direct question to Lydia. It was clear she was doing her best to come up with a reason that would have both she and her assistant coming out of this questioning intact. Were they indeed the guilty parties? If so, why? I couldn't wrap my head around the fact that Kathleen or Lydia had the wherewithal to take another person's life.

"Kathleen, maybe we should—"

"Deidre was napping when I left, and I'd really like to be back at the house before she awakens," Kathleen said, intentionally interrupting Lydia. Had she been going to explain their odd behavior and the fact that their statements weren't exactly matching up in the grand scheme of things? What caught me off guard were the tears in Kathleen's eyes, though she bowed her head as she grabbed her purse. Her resolve to hide her grief or remorse was too late. Killers usually didn't feel remorse, though, did they? I snuck a glance at Liam, and it was clear that he was weighing on whether or not to allow Kathleen to leave the shop with this hiccup in their story. "Could we maybe finish this up tomorrow?"

Kathleen had already lifted her purse off the table, completely focused on leaving the shop before anyone said another word, particularly her assistant. I had a solution to prevent her exit.

*Sweet angel of mercy, don't you dare—*

I released the pent-up energy that had harnessed in the palm of my hand, sending what wasn't weighted down on the table flying into the air. The flyers, mail, and business cards whooshed away before anyone could react, eventually landing on the greyish hardwood floor.

No one ever seemed to question when odd things like that happened, chalking it up to either a door being opened or maybe the air conditioning acting a bit wonky. People usually just immediately sprang into action to clean up the mess.

*Raven, let me remind you that we are in a shop with genuine items that descended from our ancestors. Utilizing magic around them isn't the brightest idea, if you get my drift. Oy, vey!*

"I'll get it," Liam reassured Kathleen, who had already knelt down in her black dress to try and gather up the mess of scattered papers now on the floor. He even put a reassuring hand over hers when we could both see her trembling, though the sideways look he gave me all but shouted his guess that I had something to do with the gust of wind. "Let me get this."

*While the good ol' sheriff cleans up your mess, I'll stand guard. I won't move from this spot, just in case that bell rings.*

Leo was still harping on that bell, not that I had any idea why he was so concerned about an object that every shop owner had above their door. Maybe that antihistamine had affected him more than I thought, but now seemed the perfect time for Liam and me to push Kathleen and Lydia a bit more in hopes of them finally telling us the truth.

Kathleen was in the midst of standing up somewhat shakily, giving Lydia time to whisper something frantically into her ear. The shop owner shook her head furiously, but she was unable to keep her tears at bay.

"Kathleen, you weren't at any estate auction yesterday, were you?" I asked as softly as I could, causing both women to stare at me in alarm. "You need to tell Liam what happened so that he can give your sister the closure she needs. Whatever it is that happened, Liam can help you resolve the issue."

*I wish you'd come over here and help me. Are you hearing any ringing? Anything at all? I've been staring at this bell for so long that my ears are picking up the slightest sounds. Not that I'm a dog or anything. What were the side effects of that horse pill again?*

Kathleen began to crumble right before our very eyes. It was as if she'd lost all strength after her mistake had been unmasked. She covered her face with both hands, leaving Lydia to wrap one arm around the older woman's shoulder in support. Liam stood from where he'd gathered most of the papers, observing the two women in front of him very carefully. I could sense the moment he'd made a choice on how to approach this situation.

"It wasn't our fault, Kathleen," Lydia whispered, appearing quite relieved that they were about to lift the weight of guilt off their shoulders. "It was all a big mistake. We need to tell them what happened and why we didn't come forward."

"I can't," Kathleen practically bewailed while continually shaking her head in denial. "I need to go take care of my sister."

"Kathleen, you know I can't let you do that," Liam said with full authority while still maintaining a kind tone that would hopefully give Kathleen some hope that telling the truth was the right thing to do. "It's clear you have information that can help us solve what happened to Sheriff O'Leary. The autopsy report is due back to Detective Swanson either today or tomorrow. It would be better for you to come clean now rather than later."

"Kathleen didn't intentionally hurt Pat," Lydia exclaimed, all but rushing her words together. "Neither did I. You have to believe us, Liam."

"Tell me everything, and I'll do what I can to help." Liam picked up two antique chairs that were off to the side, ushering the two women onto the fabric cushions so that they'd be more comfortable. His compassion was evident, even though there was a strong chance whatever happened in this shop was the cause of Sheriff O'Leary's death. "We'll call Detective Swanson afterward, and I'll be with you every step of the way."

*It's nice to know that the good ol' sheriff stands by his residents when the going gets tough. We might need his help one day, especially if this bell begins to ring out of the blue. Remind me to stash some extra catnip for when that time comes. Oh, and remember to see if that horse pill comes in a liquid form. I wouldn't mind sleeping through the apocalypse.*

I had a feeling that Leo wasn't talking about the squirrel apocalypse, but I could only deal with one situation at a time. Liam and I stood side by side while Lydia began to walk us through what happened on the day in question.

"Deidre had been upset for months that Pat might be having an affair with Becca Wilson. It was all she could talk about, but she refused to confront her husband or her friend," Lydia said, keeping hold of Kathleen's hand while she tried to compose herself. "You see, we had received a book on herbs and plants that contained healing properties. It mentioned that licorice oil can serve as a truth serum of sorts, so Kathleen thought she'd try it."

*Hey, I see the book she's talking about on a table back here. You should buy it. As a matter of fact, do you have your credit card? We need to buy all of this stuff. They have no idea what they've brought into their shop, and I need my beauty sleep. I can't be up all night worrying who might get their hands on some of these objects. Ohhhhh boy, I feel an asthma attack coming on.*

Considering the antihistamine would most likely prevent an asthma attack, I wasn't too worried about Leo. He seemed to have things under control on the other side of the shop, and the parts of this puzzle were finally falling into place.

"Kathleen, did you put licorice oil into Sheriff O'Leary's tea or coffee?" I asked, hoping that wasn't the case.

There was a reason I listed ingredients on all tea blends in my shop, especially after having given some out as gifts at Christmas time, only to find out that Monty had a peanut allergy. In my case, I was very lucky that Monty had an epi-pen on him at the time he'd decided to drink his favorite beverage.

*I'd rather take a liquid. I don't do needles. You know, they also have a cream you can rub on the inside of my ear for anxiety. I wonder if it comes in an edible form laced with catnip. We should ask Dr. Jameson about that the next time we see him. I could really use something like that today.*

Liam and I were still waiting for Kathleen to answer the question on whether or not she'd put a few drops of licorice oil into Sheriff O'Leary's tea or coffee. She was still crying, so Lydia answered for her.

"It was just a few drops," Lydia defended, grabbing hold of Kathleen's hand. "I was the one who read up on the different properties of plants and herbs. Kathleen bought some at some health food store and was going to take it to Deidre's house, but Pat showed up here. It was the perfect opportunity to find out if he was having an affair. We didn't want to say anything, because we had no idea if it was the licorice oil that was responsible for Pat's death. We still don't know if that's the case. Why get Deidre all upset for not reason? We wanted to wait for the autopsy report before saying a word of this to anyone. Someone else could have given Pat something to cause his death. After all, he was the sheriff. For all we know, maybe Deputy Wilson did find out about the affair and took matters into his own hands. We just didn't want to complicate things further."

*I often wonder about delusional people, especially those that reside in Paramour Bay. They put drops of an herbal oil into someone's drink moments before he dropped dead in the middle of town square…and they think someone else might have poisoned the dead sheriff?*

I also believed Kathleen and Lydia were both in denial that they played a part in a man's death, however unintentional. Who could blame them? I recall how I felt with the whole Monty situation. Luckily, he'd come out of it just fine. I couldn't imagine the guilt if something worse had happened to him.

"Did Sheriff O'Leary show any signs of being ill before he left the shop?" Liam asked, clarifying the details on the last few minutes of the man's death. "Was he having trouble breathing? Itching his skin? Grasping at his throat?"

*Hey, that sounds like me earlier today. Go figure. While we're on the subject of side effects, I'm starting to see double. That might be because I haven't taken my attention off this bell or blinked in the last ten minutes, but I thought I'd ask just in case.*

"Pat did begin to rub his chest, but I thought it was due to his heartburn," Kathleen finally managed to say, having finally gotten her emotions under control. "Like Lydia said, we were going to wait for the autopsy report before we said anything about the licorice oil. I didn't want my sister finding out that I'd tried to trick her husband into admitting his infidelity."

"By chance, did Sheriff O'Leary confess to the affair?" Liam asked, most likely just in case the licorice oil had nothing to do with the man's death.

"No, he didn't," Kathleen murmured, looking down at her hands in shame. "All Pat talked about while he was here was how much he loved Deidre. What if I am responsible for his death?"

Almost as if in response to Kathleen's question, Liam's phone chimed with an incoming call. A quick look over his shoulder revealed that Jack was calling, and most likely with the results of the autopsy. We were about to find out the cause of Sheriff O'Leary's death.

*I feel like there should be a drumroll inserted here, but I'm too worried about this bell going off. Raven, have we ever discussed cesaral spirit bells? If not, you should know that we're going to cover them in your next lesson. Who would have thought you'd get a hands-on tutorial from our local antique shop?*

# Chapter Seventeen

"WELL?" I ASKED in anticipation after Liam had disconnected the call with Jack. I couldn't imagine being in
Kathleen and Lydia's shoes. "What did the autopsy report say?"

The way Liam set his comforting gaze on the two women
said it all. I realized that we never had a true murder mystery on
our hands. It had all been a tragic accident.

Liam's call with Jack had lasted all but two or three minutes.
I'd done my best to keep Kathleen and Lydia's minds off the
outcome. During our brief discussion, I'd found that Sheriff
O'Leary had not only declared his love for Deidre, but that he'd
been planning a surprise trip for their anniversary. It was very sad
to know that he'd never get to finish seeing such a touching gift
through to the end.

*I'm hoping I get to take a trip soon. Honduras or New Zealand
would be nice. I hear the plantation tours are wonderful. The stress
of this bell is going to cause me more fur loss, and I can't afford to
lose any more tufts.*

"I really wish I could tell you a different outcome, but Sheriff
O'Leary passed away from a severe allergic reaction to licorice
oil," Liam shared grimly with the two ladies in a consoling tone.
Kathleen broke down once again, while Lydia seemed to be in
shock. "Detective Swanson should be here soon. He'll want to
question the two of you again. Tell him nothing but the truth

this time. You couldn't have known that Sheriff O'Leary was allergic to licorice oil. It was an unfortunate incident. You had no intent to do harm. However, it did result in his death and a prosecutor will have to make the final determination."

"How am I going to explain to my sister that I accidentally killed her husband?" Kathleen cried out, the usually composed woman now a complete wreck. "I'm a murderer!"

*She said it, not me.*

Lydia continued to reassure Kathleen that she was not a murderer, most likely attempting to convince herself. Kathleen was a caring woman who had wanted to protect her sister by seeking out answers in an unorthodox manner.

Would Deidre be so understanding?

"Liam," I whispered softly, tugging on his arm so that we could step to the side. I didn't want the two ladies to overhear us. "Will Jack arrest them? They didn't mean to kill Sheriff O'Leary."

*I didn't mean to find an authentic cesaral spirit bell, but here it is.*

"Jack will take their statements and confirm that there was no ill intent, though the problem arises with the fact that they withheld evidence. I honestly don't know how Jack is going to play this," Liam replied, rubbing his jawline in disbelief. "Licorice oil? Before today, I would have thought it was insane to use such a thing as truth serum. Now...well, I have a lot to learn, don't I?"

"It's true that licorice oil is one of the special components that can compel an individual to be truthful, just as other herbs and plants have healing properties." I thought back to one of my numerous lessons, grateful that I had Leo to steer me through the vast material my Nan had left behind for me to study. "

learn new things every day, Liam."

*Speaking of new things, we really need to discuss this bell and the rest of this kit.*

"Such as how to move things with your mind?" Liam asked, a hint of wariness in his tone that told me he was still grappling with this newfound knowledge. Well, he could just join the club. In all honesty, it was nice to have another person know my secret. The responsibility of such a gift could get pretty heavy at times. "That was you, right?"

I held up my right hand and wiggled my fingers.

"Elemental energy," I whispered, having leaned in a bit closer to make sure that Kathleen and Lydia didn't catch on to our topic of discussion. They were still trying to accept that their actions had cost a man's life, and I'm sure they would continue to do so for the rest of their lives. Magic and its material components were to be used with great caution. "I can harness energy in the palm of my hand."

*Well, these objects back here might actually be feeding on that energy.*

"Harness energy? In your palm?" Liam ran a hand over his face, but I had to give him credit that he didn't seem to want to run in the other direction. "This is going to be quite the education, isn't it?"

I could only smile, mainly because Liam hadn't run away from me yet.

*Give him time, Raven. I want a front row seat when you tell him about our giant Crayola, the grim reaper at the cemetery, and the local werewolf who poses as our librarian. You might want to steal the good ol' sheriff's running shoes from his closet.*

"Just think of how much help I can be in figuring out who keeps stealing lollipops off Monty's counter at the hardware store or who takes roses from Wilma's bushes out front. A little magic can go a long way, Sheriff Drake." It made me very, very happy to see the corners of Liam's lips lift at my offer to help him with his backlog of not-so-serious crimes around town. Unfortunately, he currently had to deal with the death of a colleague and the two women who were accidentally responsible. I didn't envy him this part of the job. "I need to go talk to Leo on the other side of the shop. He found some...objects. The kind that might not be such a great idea for the residents to get ahold of, if you get my drift."

Liam nodded, letting his concerned gaze land on the two women who were still seated in the chairs. He'd keep them busy while I made my way to the other side of the shop to see exactly what had Leo all worked up, because I couldn't understand how a bell could be dangerous.

*I didn't say dangerous, Raven. You really should get your ears checked out. Wax build-up can cause serious problems, you know.*

"Raven." Liam grabbed my hand before I could walk away. "I don't believe Becca Wilson was having an affair with Sheriff O'Leary. She mentioned to me that she was helping him plan a surprise trip for his wife. At first, I thought Ms. Wilson was attempting to deflect my attention away from the idea that she was having an affair. I think the reason she knew of Sheriff O'Leary's visit to Paramour Bay rather than Deputy Wilson was because the two had been talking in private about the trip beforehand."

Liam's theory made sense, especially when Becca and Claire had been chatting on the couch about hiding the evidence. They hadn't wanted Deidre to know about the surprise trip and cause her more grief in knowing that she and her husband would never be able to see it through.

I nodded my understanding, realizing how important honesty was in relationships. Sheriff O'Leary thought he'd been doing something nice for his wife, all the while that she thought his sneaking around had been due to his interest in another woman. He loved her, yet his wife had spent the last few months of his life believing that he had betrayed her.

"Thank you," Liam said, squeezing my hand in gratitude. "Thank you for trusting me with the truth, Raven."

*Okay. Can we cut the sappy stuff, please? We have the potential of facing a supernatural apocalypse if we don't take precautions here. Now really isn't the time to get all emotional, Raven.*

I sighed in reluctance to part with Liam after such a revelation about our relationship, but I also couldn't have us on the verge of a supernatural apocalypse.

"What is it that has you..." I let my whisper trail off as I finally saw the table in question. It was a good thing that this section was out of sight from the others, because I could only imagine my expression of horror. "Oh, this is bad, Leo. Is that a black mass candle? I mean, one that has been ritually deconsecrated?"

*Yes.*

"Is that a triple moon pentacle offering bowl?" I asked in disbelief, hoping I was wrong. "And an athame dagger?"

*Double yes.*

"And the altar tile? Is that the one from..."

*Sweet angel of mercy, yes! Yes, yes, yes! All of these things are from the official log of evidence presented at the Salem witch trials. They are all magical relics. I hope you have a lot of room on your credit card, Raven. These are dangerous objects to have in the hands of humans. They need to be removed from here immediately, if not sooner.*

"Now would probably be a good time for you to tell me what a cesaral spirit bell is used for," I whispered, afraid to touch any of these items. I leaned back a bit to make sure that Liam was still talking to Kathleen and Lydia. Sure enough, they were still at the other end of the shop. I breathed a bit easier, though we still had the problem of buying all of these objects and hauling them to the cottage. "It doesn't summon evil spirits, does it?"

*No, but it does warn the owner of when an ethereal spirit is near.*

"That's a good thing, right?"

*Well, only if that spirit isn't evil, of course. I figure as long as it doesn't ring, we're in good shape.*

A bit of tension released from my shoulders. We'd already dealt with the spirits of Mazie and Lucille, promptly sending them back through the veil from whence they came. Job accomplished, and no one from the other side had paid us a visit recently.

"Good," I said with a quick nod, feeling a bit better. "I mean, what are the odds of that thing going off anyway? A million to one?"

Leo and I were always warning each other about jinxing our odds or basically alerting karma to our precipitous presence, but my attempt at reassuring the both of us that Paramour Bay was spirit-free had backfired on us once again.

The bell rang…loud and clear.

*I'll take another horse pill now.*

We both stared at the old relic in horror when it rang once more.

*Make that a double, Raven.*

~ THE END ~

*Get ready for a spine-tingling cozy mystery that has ghosts, ghouls, and goblins coming out of the woodwork in the next spirited installment of the Paramour Bay Mysteries by USA Today Bestselling Author Kennedy Layne...*

Grab your copy of Spirited Blend!
kennedylayne.com/spirited-blend.html

Mounds of delicious candy corn, jack-o-lanterns, and spooky hayrides are all part of this year's Halloween festivities in Paramour Bay. Raven Marigold plans to make the most out of this All Hallows' Eve, which just so happens to be her birthday.

Not everyone in town seems to have gotten the festive memo, though. One of the residents is claiming that the spirit of her dead husband has been paying her nocturnal visits, while other townsfolk are making similar claims about their deceased relatives. Is this someone's version of a supernatural flash mob or has someone accidentally pierced the veil to the afterlife?

It's going to be a hauntingly good time in this quaint coastal town, so bring along your lanterns and flashlights as Raven and the gang take a midnight stroll through the local cemetery to try and solve this hair-raising mystery!

# Books by Kennedy Layne

## Hex on Me Mysteries
If the Curse Fits
Cursing up the Wrong Tree
The Squeaky Ghost Gets the Curse
The Curse that Bites

## Paramour Bay Mysteries
Magical Blend
Bewitching Blend
Enchanting Blend
Haunting Blend
Charming Blend
Spellbinding Blend
Cryptic Blend
Broomstick Blend
Spirited Blend

## Office Roulette Series
Means (Office Roulette, Book One)
Motive (Office Roulette, Book Two)
Opportunity (Office Roulette, Book Three)

## Keys to Love Series
Unlocking Fear (Keys to Love, Book One)
Unlocking Secrets (Keys to Love, Book Two)
Unlocking Lies (Keys to Love, Book Three)
Unlocking Shadows (Keys to Love, Book Four)
Unlocking Darkness (Keys to Love, Book Five)

## About the Author

First and foremost, I love life. I love that I'm a wife, mother, daughter, sister… and a writer.

I am one of the lucky women in this world who gets to do what makes them happy. As long as I have a cup of coffee (maybe two or three) and my laptop, the stories evolve themselves and I try to do them justice. I draw my inspiration from a retired Marine Master Sergeant that swept me off of my feet and has drawn me into a world that fulfills all of my deepest and darkest desires. Erotic romance, military men, intrigue, with a little bit of kinky chili pepper (his recipe), fill my head and there is nothing more satisfying than making the hero and heroine fulfill their destinies.

Thank you for having joined me on their journeys…

Email: kennedylayneauthor@gmail.com

Facebook: facebook.com/kennedy.layne.94

Twitter: twitter.com/KennedyL_Author

Website: www.kennedylayne.com

Newsletter:
www.kennedylayne.com/aboutnewsletter.html

Made in the USA
Coppell, TX
30 October 2021